In the Spirit of McPhineas Lata

and Other Stories

In the Spirit of McPhineas Lata

and Other Stories

Lauri Kubuitsile

By the Same Author

Children's Books:
Mmele and the Magic Bones
Lorato and the Wire Car
Birthday Wishes and Other Stories
The Curse of the Gold Coins Signed
Hopelessly in Love

Short Story Collections for Children (Co-written with
Wame Molefhe and Bontekanye Botumile):
No One is Alone
The Ram He Brings a Message

Romance:
Kwaito Love
Can He Be the One
Mr Not Quite Good Enough
Love in the Shadows

Books in the Kate Gomolemo Detective Series:
The Fatal Payout
Murder for Profit
Anything for Money
Claws of a Killer

Publication © Hands-On Books 2012
Text © Lauri Kubuitsile 2012

P O Box 385, Athlone, 7760, South Africa
modjaji.books@gmail.com
http://modjaji.book.co.za

ISBN 978-1-920590-34-5

Book and cover design: Natascha Mostert
Cover photograph: Graham Commeford
Printed and bound by Mega Digital, Cape Town
Set in Garamond

ebook edition first published in 2011 by HopeRoad Publishing
PO Box 55544, Exhibition Road, London, SW7 2DB
www.hoperoadpublishing.com

To LSK
As always

Contents

Eddie Fisher Won't Be Coming in Today

VIVA MAINA arrived that day at the tail-end of a dust storm. As the empty Simba chip packets settled back in the branches of the leafless hedge at the school gate, out of the grey dust she appeared. I sat on the lid of the dustbin outside of the airless staffroom smoking a cigarette and as she emerged I felt my heart shift in my chest and knew from the look of her we were in for something.

'I'm looking for the headmaster,' she said, holding each word a fraction of a second too long in her mouth, caressing it with her tongue before letting it loose into the air to be gobbled up by my waiting ears. My eyes rested on her lips – full and hibiscus red, her eyes – dark and deep, and her body – thin-waisted and broad come-hither hips. I was lost in her physical being and just as I began to drift away into Viva Maina fantasyland, a place where I was to spend an inordinate amount of time in during the coming weeks, I was pulled back into reality by the cigarette burning my fingers. Throwing it to the ground, I said, 'He's inside. Should I take you?'

The words she spoke to me that day were rare gems, but I didn't know that then. Viva Maina, we would to come to realise, was not big on conversation. It wasn't that she was a snob, she just had no interest in speaking to anyone or hearing anything anyone had to say to her. Viva Maina seemed perfectly content in her own mind. Her presence, though, caused a lot of noise as the huge block of lusty, Viva-inspired dreams from a school full of male teachers and puberty-entrapped boys needed space. It squeezed into the dust-covered little patch of matchbox teachers' houses and dilapidated student hostels causing loud squeaks and groans and complaints of 'move over'. It bent things that, in the end I realised, should never have been bent.

Viva Maina hardly spoke, that is, until she met Eddie Fisher. Of all of the men she could have chosen, why Eddie Fisher, no one knew. Mudongo stood up in the staffroom, full of indignation, when it became clear he would not be the one. 'Look at me for God's sake.' Heads bobbed in agreement. Without a doubt he was the best looking among us. We all knew it, but Viva Maina seemed to have overlooked that fact.

'And at least I have money,' Loago lamented from the corner – he was the only one at the school with a working car.

But she chose Eddie Fisher. Eddie Fisher with the blue-checked shirts for Monday, Wednesday and Friday and the red for Tuesday and Thursday. Eddie Fisher who was as tall as most form one boys and so thin that most of those boys could have lifted him over their heads if they'd dared. We all had to admit that he did have two perfectly sculpted ears and a lovely smile, though few had seen much of it before Viva Maina showed up. Smiling had not been a big part of Eddie Fisher's life up until then and that was primarily because of Thelma.

The unseen Thelma was a voice echoing nightly through the paths and around the corners of the teachers' quarters, causing hair to stand on end and planting seeds for horrific nightmares. 'What are you doing now, Eddie Fisher?' it would question in a tone set aside for ghouls and goblins.

'I've seen her,' Loago would tell people. 'She's as wide and as tall as the doorframe. Her massive breasts nearly touch the floor. That day I saw her, she pulled Eddie Fisher, gasping for air, out from under one of them.'

Though the men in the staffroom listened with all seriousness, they knew Loago's story couldn't be trusted; nobody's Thelma stories could. And there were many stories at that school at the edge of the desert. Rumour had it that once a week, a whole night was spent swapping and comparing the latest stories about Eddie Fisher's wife at the boys' hostels.

Sometimes she was tiny, with her flesh like biltong holding tightly to her cranky bones, or round and short, with angry eyebrows sharp as knives. Sometimes she was a sex-starved nymphomaniac who'd been known to snatch up boys who'd let their minds and steps wander, drifting too close to the house's front door. Other times she was a cold fish who tossed poor Eddie Fisher to the ground if he spied her out of the corner of his lust-filled eye. Though the stories moved up and down and left and right, everybody agreed on one thing: Eddie Fisher had a seriously hard-luck life.

At least until Viva Maina arrived.

Viva spotted Eddie after a week, and from then on they were always together, except when he disappeared into Thelma's house, followed by a 'Where've you been, Eddie Fisher?' ringing through the school. The staff kept an eye on Viva and Eddie as they snuck away to sit under the big camel thorn tree near the science laboratory. Once there Viva Maina talked and laughed, throwing her head back and her long shapely leg forward with abandon. Eddie Fisher would giggle into his hand and smile and smile at Viva.

'What could they even be talking about?' Mudongo asked, peering from the corner of the staffroom window.

'I know Eddie likes reading. Maybe they're talking about books,' I tried, knowing by the look of them, books were not the topic of conversation.

Viva reached her hand forward and with her long finger slowly traced the edge of Eddie's shapely ear. The staffroom let out a painful sigh. It was too much for Loago. 'Damn that Eddie Fisher! Damn him to hell!' And he pulled the curtain shut and, with one look of his dagger eyes, dared anyone to open them again.

I wasn't jealous of Eddie Fisher. I'd heard the bellows of Thelma and had spent the past two years watching Eddie creep around the school, trying his best to stay unnoticed. The story went that he'd been posted at the school when it started five years previously and that a clerk at TSM in Gaborone, 800-odd kilometres away, had thrown his blue file deep at the back of a cabinet, never to be found again, when Thelma bellowed into her face about how she was not going be moving out to the desert. Thanks to Thelma, Eddie was now permanent and pensionable in this forgotten windswept corner of Botswana. No, I couldn't slight Eddie Fisher, he hadn't brought Viva Maina to him: she had come of her own volition. A drop of good luck after a deluge of bad.

Three weeks after Viva's arrival, Eddie went missing. I was sitting in my usual place on the dustbin lid, trying to find a breath of fresh air in the stagnant heat that engulfed us, when Viva rushed up. 'Where's Eddie Fisher?'

I shrugged my shoulders. I was among the unhappy ones, the unchosen, and now I had the opportunity to let her know my view on that situation.

'He's not come to school today,' she said. 'I think she's keeping him in.' Her lovely smooth skin was flushed, and in her frantic state, she forgot to close her lips completely when she was done speaking and my mind drifted away, thinking of that slight open space.

'Someone must go and ask Thelma.'

I was yanked back rudely. 'Ask Thelma?' The sun had addled her, I concluded.

In frustration she left, running for the staffroom. She managed to collect Loago, a youngster named Jakes, and the always willing Mudongo. I trailed behind them, hoping I might get a peep at the elusive Thelma, but not willing to be at the front in case her eyes threw radioactivity or her piercing voice caused permanent damage to my hearing. I was interested, but no hero.

The small parade headed down the dusty drive, under the baking noon sun, along the back of the teachers' quarters to the tin-roofed house occupied by Eddie and Thelma Fisher. Loago, at the front, gave a quick look back at us, trying to show he had no fear and then knocked without much conviction on the metal door. When it opened, he jumped back. From the darkness, a voice bellowed, 'Eddie Fisher won't be coming in today.'

The door slammed shut and we backed away, not sure of what we'd seen or hadn't seen. We moved away quickly, despite the worried pleas of Viva Maina.

Thelma was right. Eddie Fisher didn't come in that day or the next day or the one after that. He never came to school again. Discussion was rampant as to what had happened.

'She killed him. I know it,' Mudongo insisted.

'Maybe, but then what?' I asked. 'What'd she do with the body?'

'Who knows with Thelma?' Loago asked, shrugging his shoulders. 'Maybe she ate him.' He threw a card down from the tattered stack in his hand and, though he didn't seem to be playing any card game in particular, looked annoyed at what the card revealed and picked them all up in resignation and began shuffling the deck again. 'Thelma had enough of Eddie and Viva and put an end to it the only way she could.'

The disappearance took its toll on Viva Maina. As time passed, she began to talk to the absent Eddie, walking around the school grounds with him even though he was nothing but a patch of air next to her where he should have been. Like most things at that school in the desert, we got used to it. Like the ghoulish shouts of the enigmatic Thelma, and the missing Eddie Fisher, the beautiful, mad Viva Maina became a part of our lives, living side by side with the dust storms and the relentless desert heat as the days passed and Eddie Fisher became more and more absent.

Then one day a moving truck pulled up to Eddie Fisher's house. Crowding at the staffroom window, we watched the men move back and forth between the truck and the house carrying surprisingly ordinary things: sofas, tables, a bed. I saw Viva Maina standing at the edge of the teachers' quarters, her hands hanging at her sides, waiting to see what would come out of that house, if Eddie would be part of the household contents.

When the moving men were finished, a shadow moved at the front of the door, and everyone became silent. The time had come. We were finally going to know the truth about Eddie Fisher's wife and possible killer. I held my breath, and I was not alone because the air in the staffroom had become still with the lack of respiration. And suddenly there she was. She was not big nor small, she was not old nor very young, nor ugly, nor beautiful. She wore a nondescript dress and a doek on her head. She had neither fangs nor claws.

'Well *that's* an anticlimax,' Mudongo said a fraction of a second too soon, because then Thelma saw Viva Maina standing waiting for her Eddie Fisher to finally re-emerge from the house where he'd last been seen.

'What do you want, girl?' Thelma boomed and I covered my ears involuntarily, wondering how Viva, who was much closer to the horrible sound, continued to stand exactly as she had, arms hanging at her side, her ears unprotected.

'I want to say goodbye to Eddie Fisher,' Viva said, and the staffroom oohed at her bravery.

Thelma took a few steps toward Viva and we shivered in fear, imagining that Thelma was planning to break Viva in two. But then she stopped. She looked at Viva with eyes black as tar and then threw her head back and laughed. It was a laugh so devoid of happiness or joy it made the lone camel thorn tree shrink back a few inches, and the people listening to suddenly think about the graves of loved ones, puppies smashed flat under car tyres and tiny coffins made for babies. It was the worst of life disguised inside a bright yellow balloon; terrible trickery. The laugh hung in the hot, dust-laden air as Thelma went to the truck, pulled herself inside and they drove away.

As soon as the moving truck was out of the school gate, Viva ran straight for Eddie Fisher's house. 'Eddie!' she shouted into the open door. 'Eddie!' she shouted into the corners of the empty sitting-room. 'Eddie!' she shouted at the crushed Coke tin lying in the dirty corner where the marks on the tiles showed a refrigerator had stood.

I followed in behind her, hoping to capitalise on her final despair. 'He's not here. He's gone, Viva. Eddie Fisher is gone.' I held out my arms and she ran straight past them without a word, out of the door and towards the desert. I turned and ran after her, but stopped at the edge of the school compound. In 50°C heat, beautiful Viva Maina or not, I was not stepping out into that. She'd come back and I'd be waiting.

But she didn't.

Days passed. Students were grouped into search parties led by a teacher, sent out into the desert once the sun had lowered a bit. Contingents went out each day and returned, but Viva Maina was nowhere to be found. Her tracks crissed and crossed like a drunk staggering home after a binge, but they led nowhere. After five days, we accepted the inevitable. Viva Maina was dead.

'It wasn't meant to last,' Mudongo said philosophically.

'And what's that supposed to mean?' Loago asked, inexplicably annoyed.

'I mean Viva. You can't bring a person like that out here without something giving.'

I looked at Mudongo and considered what he'd said. Maybe he was right. Still, I couldn't shake the mystery of it. Where did Eddie Fisher go? Where was Viva? And what did Thelma know?

I was lucky because just before I'd fallen into the suspended animation of the despair of the forgotten, I was transferred back to the world of the living. I was lucky to get a place in the north, in the city of Francistown, full of plenty of women so that a Viva Maina or two caused no disturbances or dangers. Life was back to normal and I'd nearly forgotten all about Eddie Fisher and Viva Maina and their mysterious disappearances.

I had new things to occupy my time. I was in love. I was in love with the pretty, calm Lorato. I'd learnt my lesson from a distance; passionate, wild, reckless love was dangerous. I would settle for the tranquil breeze of love lightly touching me here and there, harming no one, as offered by Lorato.

We were walking home from the cinema one cool winter evening when she told me about a new woman who'd come to work with her at the council office where she was employed as a social worker.

'She's beautiful, but there's something about her,' Lorato said.

I was only listening with half my mind; the other half was wondering how I could convince Lorato that despite her having to get up for work the next morning, she should spend the night at my small flat. 'What's wrong with her?' I asked absent-mindedly.

'You know Tshenolo Rebone, that tall, thin awkward one who runs the computer department?' she asked.

I brought my mind back to the conversation. 'Yeah, I know him.'

'So this woman is suddenly attracted to him. Him of all people. She's beautiful, with these amazing eyes and curving hips, and she speaks in this slow odd way. I just don't get it.' Lorato shook her head at the strangeness of it. 'Anyway, Viva's also a bit strange, hardly says a word to anyone but Tshenolo. A bit stuck on herself maybe.'

I stopped walking and grabbed Lorato by the sides of her face, yanking her head towards me. 'What did you say her name was?'

'Ouch! You're hurting me. What's wrong with you?' Lorato pulled away and stood at some distance from me with a look in her eye that questioned my sanity. 'She's called Viva, Viva Maina.'

'You're lying. Why are you saying that?'

'What do you mean, I'm lying? That's her name. Why would I lie? What is wrong with you?' She started walking away angrily.

I ran after her. 'I'm sorry. It's just … I knew a Viva, a Viva Maina. I thought she was dead.'

The next day I skipped work and malingered around Lorato's office, waiting for Viva to emerge. It was past the lunch-hour rush and I still hadn't seen her. I dodged Lorato coming back from lunch with a group of her office mates by ducking into a nearby Chinese shop, hiding behind a rack of clothes smelling of mothballs, ignoring the shouts of 'What you want here?' from the tiny, fierce old lady who threatened me with a plastic fly-swatter.

Just as the last latecomers entered the building, I saw Viva sitting on a nearby bench with Tshenolo from Lorato's office. I couldn't believe my eyes! It was her. She had survived the desert and the loss of Eddie Fisher and now she was happily in love again. I wanted to go up to her, but something stopped me. I watched her kiss Tshenolo and then run her fingers along his neck, and my stomach jumped. I thought again about ruining her happiness with my unhappy Eddie Fisher baggage. Though I was curious about how she had survived and where she had made off to that day, I couldn't interrupt her happiness with my curiosity. I took one last look at her and walked away.

I never mentioned Viva again and Lorato never brought her up. I got the impression she thought Viva had been one of my old girlfriends, and I sort of liked that she thought that, so we all kept quiet, keeping our Viva thoughts to ourselves.

It was a spring day, sparkling and bright after an early morning shower. Lorato and I were walking to the nearby park to eat our takeaway lunch of fried chicken. I was thinking about how, when we sat down on the park bench, I would talk to Lorato about serious things, about marriage and children. I had decided it was time to get things moving in that direction. Today was the day; this shiny spring day would be the day my life would take a new turn.

We found a bench in the shade and I bent down to wipe the stray raindrops off with one of the serviettes. 'You won't believe what has happened,' Lorato said, sitting down and unpacking the chicken and chips inside the bag, placing them carefully on the bench between us. 'Tshenolo has gone missing.'

My heart stopped and I said a bit too sharply, 'Missing? What about Viva?'

Lorato took a bite of chicken and chewed and swallowed it as I waited the seconds for her answer. 'She's beside herself with worry. He hasn't been to work all week. Disappeared into thin air, it seems.'

I sat back on the bench and forgot all about my plans of marriage and children. I forgot about chicken. I forgot about everything. As Lorato's voice asked from far away in the distance, 'Are you okay?', all I could see in front of me was the beautiful Viva appearing out of the dust, that day so long ago at the school at the edge of the desert, appearing out of the dust like an apparition, looking for the headmaster but, I realised now, in search of something altogether different.

Pulane's Eyes

DESPITE FORTY-SEVEN years of waiting, her mother, surprisingly, took no notice of Pulane's passage into the world from between her tired legs. It wasn't that she hadn't been waiting for her first child to arrive, because she had. It was because she had just walked the considerable distance to the midwife's house and found her not at home, and was in the middle of one of her mythical rants. Only when she stopped for a breath to let a little more air in to propel her angry words into the cosmos, did she notice Pulane, who had made her bumpy arrival from vagina to floor without a sound. Her mother stopped in mid-rant, pulled up her skirt and looked down at the baby, who looked back with questioning eyes; eyes that wondered if it had been the right thing to come back to the world through the legs of this woman who had given her birth no notice at all.

Notwithstanding her initial distraction, Pulane's mother was overjoyed that the long childless drought she had endured, losing three husbands along the way because of it, had finally ended. She picked up the infant from between her legs, put her nose up to her and took a big, hearty sniff; as she expected, the baby smelt of the first fat drops of rain after a long drought. Her scent was wet and dusty. The girl's passage cleared away the dirt along the path, dirt and dust that had prevented the drops from falling. Her mother smiled at the baby. 'Pulane,' she christened her without any consultation, much against custom, though she had no fear, for she knew now she was free and clear.

She was right, too. By the time she reached the end of her fertility, at the age of fifty-six, she had seven babies that followed the same path into the world as Pulane had, one right after the other in a quick, efficient procession. Thanks to Pulane, her infertile mother, tossed aside by so many as worthless, was soon swooning with fertility.

Pulane grew up as the cherished one. Everyone knew she was the miracle child who had burst open MmaPulane's womb. Pulane was passed from hands to loving hands. She was anointed with sweet-smelling oils and fed tasty treats. Pulane's questioning, untrusting eyes watched all the love that was lavished on her and wondered, 'What do they want from me?'

It was true that some were smoothing Pulane's dresses and feeding her with the finest chocolates only because they wanted something for themselves. Some wanted a favour from MmaPulane, who had made a name for herself by using her rants to force people to her position. Often the people acquiesced only to get her to shut up. People sought her rants for unyielding building inspectors or police officers with too much faith in the rule of law. So, they rained goodies on Pulane, hoping that the backsplash would knock against her mother.

But those were in the minority. The bulk of Pulane's admirers were looking for her well-publicised powers of fertility. *Radio Mall* had spread to all corners of the country the fact that Pulane had opened up the path from her mother's broken womb and got things flowing again. So, the infertile arrived bearing shiny dolls with yellow plastic hair and hats made from soft impala leather. They hoped to get some help from the little girl. Pulane looked at all of them with her sceptical eyes until they could tolerate their endless, silent asking no longer and the people slumped back home. Some cured, some not, all decided in their minds, regardless of her powers to cure infertility, that Pulane was a highly untrusting sort.

Entle's curse was that she was born beautiful. To compound this genetic bad luck, she found herself smack in the middle of a family who, in one generation, had progressed from living in a mud rondaval thatched with grass to a three-storey mansion with gold taps and Italian tiles, located in the fashionable Gaborone North suburbs. The merging of hereditary and environmental factors meant that Entle was raised in an insulated vacuum. It was agreed, without her consultation, long before she'd grown enough wits in her skull to have an opinion, that the beautiful Entle would grow up to marry a rich, handsome man and the legacy of her family would be firmly established. Such things don't need to be discussed, once decided; actions put them into motion and shared intentions ensure success.

So, though Entle went to school and excelled in writing magical, mysterious poetry and calculating even the most complex of sums, none of that was of any interest to her family. It was handy only in that it kept Entle busy while allowing nature to prepare her body for its inevitable role – to attract the rich, handsome husband and to give birth to tiny beautiful heirs to his fortune.

The plan, sadly, went astray. Entle attracted the rich, handsome husband, son to a Motswana diamond mine owner and his Australian wife, but after that things started to veer off course. The husband, Kgosi, began to squirm and squeal as years passed by and no children were produced.

At first his complaints fell only on the pearly white ears of his Australian mother, who paid them little notice. She was not keen on being a grandmother, since her thin, fashionable figure and Botoxed smooth face still ensured her a steady stream of young, fit men to cavort with. 'Grandmother' was not a tag she wanted anywhere in the vicinity of her name, for fear the word would get out and the healthy stream would dry up forever. So Kgosi whined and groaned and his mother's response was invariably, 'Does my bum look big in this?'

As years passed, Kgosi could contain his complaints no longer and so he took them to Entle's parents. Since they were, at heart, good, traditional Batswana parents, they trembled at their son-in-law's complaint for they knew the disaster that would ensue if Entle didn't get to work producing some children. A wife sent back to her parents was an embarrassment few could withstand.

MmaEntle spoke quietly to her close associates. They told her of a woman, in the north, in the fingers of the

Delta, who could help MmaEntle's daughter. She was a wily, untrusting woman, but she'd opened up the wombs of many, including her own mother, and, if Entle could be saved, this woman would be the one to do it.

So, Entle was piled into the big, rudely expensive SUV, along with her mother and the close associates, and they hit the A1 heading north. They stopped along the way to sleep in expensive hotels and to eat the food of the wealthy, which happily lodged itself in their narrowing arteries. Finally, after three days of travelling, they arrived in the village at the end of one of the fingers of the Delta and searched out the house of the old woman they called Pulane.

Pulane, with her searching eyes, had grown up to be a woman who could trust no one completely. Her untrusting nature kept men away, so she never had any children of her own. She built a house down the dirt road from her mother's, a distance close enough to hear her mother's still-healthy rants. Her mother's house was filled with her children and their children, and was just beginning to overflow with their children's children.

Pulane, instead, filled her house with cats, since cats never expected anyone to trust them in the first place, so in return were willing to accept conditional love, the only kind Pulane had on offer. She filled her days reading and weaving beautiful cloth pictures on the big loom she placed in the sunniest sitting-room of her house. The visits from infertile strangers had lessened; they trickled in about two per day. About three a week came back to give her money or presents as a show of thanks for solving their problem.

The loom itself had been one of these presents from a couple who had travelled all the way from Bulawayo in search of a baby. When the baby arrived, they called Pulane and asked her what she would like in return. She was surprised to hear the answer coming from her lips, but when the loom arrived it filled a pocket of space in her life that she hadn't known was there. She started weaving her pictures straight away. She had a talent for it and pictures flowed from her head to the wool stretched across the loom. Beautiful pictures of happy families and women climbing mountains, trees blowing free in the wind and flowers turning to the sun. She kept buckets and buckets of every colour of wool imaginable, as she was very careful to get the colours of things just right. Nowadays, when a couple pitched up looking for a baby, they often left with one of Pulane's cloth paintings.

That day, she was sitting at her loom, starting a new painting, just beginning to prepare the warp. She was threading crimson-red wool through the heddle when MmaEntle and her entourage arrived. The cats heard the car first and jumped from their positions on the loom, where they watched Pulane at work, up to the tops of the bookshelves. All five – for there were five cats in total, two full black, three completely white – sat like fat balls of fur, their feet tucked tidily under their bodies, equally placed along the tops of the bookshelves, watching.

'Ko! Ko!' MmaEntle said at the open door.

Pulane didn't get up from her loom. She continued moving the ball of red wool back and forth through the slots, but she shouted out, 'Tsena!'

MmaEntle and her two associates greeted the tall, strong, grey-dreadlocked Pulane, who turned to them as they entered. She looked at the women. She saw that they were rich and probably panic-stricken by things not going according to their plan. Rich people were like that. Poor people were far more accepting of problems, maybe because they had lots more of them to contend with. She suspected these rich people's problem involved the young, beautiful woman who hovered in the doorway, eyeing Pulane's many buckets of coloured wool.

'Come in. It's bad luck to stand in a doorway. That's where the goblins live,' Pulane called to Entle, who quickly stepped into the wide, breezy sitting-room. She turned back and inspected the edges of the door-frame for any evidence of Pulane's assertion, but she saw nothing except a few spots of peeled paint. Not knowing much about the behaviour of goblins, she wondered if she should be concerned by the absent paint. Entle had grown into a woman prone to mental vacations from a life that bored her to distraction, and soon she was whirling around in a world of goblins who climbed into people's lives through spots where the paint had chipped away, allowing them a clear way out of the door-frames in which they customarily lived. That was why she hadn't heard her mother.

'Entle!' her mother shouted for the third time, pulling Entle's mind back into the room filled with wool.

'Mme?' she responded.

'Come here and lie on this bed, so Miss Pulane can have a look at you.'

Entle walked to the bed and lay down. MmaEntle had got it slightly wrong. Pulane didn't actually look at her patients, not anymore. Over the years, she'd learnt a better method of helping the people that came to her. She held her hands a few centimetres over the womb and waited. She waited to feel the warmth, for all wombs give off a natural warmth caused by their creative powers. As her hands hovered over a woman's womb, the warmth spread up through Pulane's hands and arms. It filled her body and hummed all the way down to her feet. The warmth made its way through all the parts of her body and then slowly retreated back to its rightful place. And then it was a matter of 'wait and see'. Sometimes it worked the first time. Sometimes on the second. If it hadn't worked by the third time, then it was not going to work at all and it was better if the woman moved her thoughts away from being a mother and got on with other projects.

Entle lay cooperatively on the bed while Pulane held her hands above her. She looked around at the cloth paintings on the walls. The colours were bright and varied. Where a blue was needed, there might be a few patches of sky blue, another nearby would have darkened a shade to cerulean, fading into teal, and then darkening further to navy and in another spot cornflower. The colours massaged Entle's eyes and the relief of it pulled her away again so that she hadn't realised everything was finished and it was time to leave.

Pulane wondered what this young, beautiful woman wanted from her life, but she discovered nothing hidden in her eyes. From what she could see, though, it was clear that the unwilling children were most needed by the rich mother and her associates. What this beautiful young woman wanted was a puzzle that would trouble Pulane during the two months' wait before Entle and her mother drove the distance to the edge of the Okavango once again in search of a baby.

Kgosi was full of love when Entle returned the first time from Pulane. He swept her into their bedroom and hammered away while Entle lay on her back with a slight smile on her lips, dreaming about colours. To keep her mind from swirling completely away, she restricted her fantasies to one colour at a time.

On that day, while Kgosi worked so hard at planting his seed, Entle was thinking about yellow. She tasted the tanginess of chartreuse and felt the dusty edge of goldenrod while rolling in the warm glow of amber; lost completely in her yellow world.

Kgosi toppled off her in a collapse of breath and body. He gave her the perfunctory kiss on the cheek and then rushed to the hot, soapy shower he required immediately after sex. Entle turned on her side, the barren seeds Kgosi had so dutifully implanted in her body dripping slowly down her thigh, just as she finished with yellow and drifted smoothly on to green. Jade. Kelly. Lime. Olive. Shamrock.

When blood appeared again on the second month after the visit to Pulane, Kgosi raged, 'If you don't get yourself sorted out this time – don't come back!'

He was raised as a beautiful, rich, spoilt boy and so could not understand why he could not have exactly what he wanted. If Entle couldn't give him what he demanded, someone else would, or so he thought.

Entle was not that concerned. A thrown-away wife was an ignored woman, a non-person that no one cared about. No care meant no attention, no opinions and, Entle realised, this would mean that, for the first time in her life, she would be free of the life-plan created by others for the baby born rich and beautiful all those years ago. All of their wants and wishes would crash and burn, leaving her only the cherished ashes. Secretly, she celebrated.

Kgosi contacted MmaEntle and informed her of what he had decided. MmaEntle rushed to the couple's too-big house and collected her daughter. She decided it was best to leave the associates behind this time. She'd begun to wonder if they might very well be the problem; close friends or not, jealousy was a powerful emotion and she wouldn't put it past them to make deals with traditional doctors to ensure her daughter remained barren.

They arrived at Pulane's just as the old lady was removing her latest cloth painting from the loom. Entle stood in the expansive sitting-room and let her eyes wander the length of the painting. It was of two people entwined. The way they were entangled made it hard to see which leg belonged with which body, which hand with which arm. They were individually lost in their togetherness. The colours were variations of brown, a hundred different shades making shadows and light in the strands of wool woven in and out of each other. Entle smiled.

Pulane put the painting aside and asked Entle to lie down on the bed, as before. Entle walked to the bed and sat on the edge of it. Before lying back, she carefully reached into her pocket and pulled out three short lengths of wool. The first was dyed the rich, red brown of burnt sienna, the middle one a flat, pale ecru, while the third was just a shade redder than the first, an earthy carmine. Entle held out her hand to Pulane.

'What is that?' MmaEntle asked from the corner where she stood. She looked at the bits of wool and ordered, 'Entle, lie back and stop playing with those strings. You're not taking this seriously at all.' She looked to Pulane for back-up, but the strange woman offered her nothing.

Pulane reached for the three pieces of wool. She held them up to the sunlight and let the colours radiate. She looked back at Entle, her eyes flat and sparkling, with not a single question bouncing around in them. The cats, like moving dice, three whites with two black dots mixed between them, climbed carefully down from the bookshelves to get a closer look at what was happening.

Entle lay back and Pulane held her hands over her womb. The warmth moved from Entle through Pulane's body and back to its rightful place. After some moments, Pulane turned to MmaEntle. 'I think this time she should remain behind.'

'Remain behind?' MmaEntle asked, confused. 'For how long?'

Entle sat up on the side of the bed. She looked around the room full of light and colour. She thought she was going to like building a new life from scratch here with the five cats and the questioning eyes of Pulane.

'How long?' Pulane repeated, rolling the words around her mouth for a few moments. She looked down at the three perfectly dyed brown pieces of wool and pushed them around the palm of her hand with her long finger. 'For as long as it takes.'

Funny Rich Man

No MATTER the business, he used Old English font, fire engine red, with a white background. There was no need for discussion because everyone knew. If you wanted a sign done, you called Rre Kopang. He'd pull up on his black Humber bicycle, with paint, thinners and brushes in an orange milk crate strapped to the back with two yellow and green bungee cords, his skeletal dog, *Tau,* trailing behind. The only question to be asked once he arrived was 'What size?' You could choose big or small. Discussions over, he got straight to work.

This was how the village of Lephaleng came to look the way it did. A to Z Electronics, Rest in Peace Funeral Home, Stop By Bar, Go Siame Supermarket: all had signs out in front of the business establishment in red writing with white backgrounds, the intricate, hand-drawn Old English font giving no indication as to what could be found inside.

When asked about his predilection, Rre Kopang would say, 'It's the writing wa ga Mmamosadinyana.' Mmamosadinyana – the British Queen. RreKopang had been a staunch supporter of Mmamosadinyana, a staunch supporter ever since he'd worn the uniform for her in WWII. For him, every sign was a tribute to Her Majesty.

Beyond his love of the English, little was known about the tall, thin, ageless, white-haired sign painter. His only companion, Tau, was close-lipped on how they occupied their time when not painting signs. People in the village would shake their heads and mumble, 'He's funny, very funny.'

That funny took on a whole new meaning when Rre Kopang passed away. Mr Mohammed, the owner of Star Bed and Breakfast, in urgent need of a new sign, had waited the whole morning and half of the afternoon before sending Kago, his assistant manager, out in the Hilux to see what was keeping the old man. Kago found Tau in a state, pacing up and down in the tiny compound. He opened the unlocked door to the one-roomed house and, though he was for a moment distracted by the many pictures of Mmamosadinyana that filled the unpainted cement walls, Kago soon realised that Rre Kopang, though appearing peacefully asleep on the bed, was decidedly dead.

Since no one knew of any relatives, the neighbour women streamed in to take control of the situation and that was when the trunk was found: a large, beautifully carved sandalwood trunk packed full of P100 bills, a million pula solid and clean, money saved over the years from his ubiquitous sign painting, at least that's what was decided, for nobody knew for sure. A note on top said, 'For the care of Tau'. Though the village was not keen on spending a million pula on a dog, the kgosi insisted that Rre Kopang's wishes be abided by. And so, the dog of the funny, rich man who loved the Queen and made hundreds of signs in her honour ended its days living like royalty.

A Shift in the Wind

MAYBE IT was the updraft that pushed empty plastic bags high into the sky to dance around in the sunlight with a never-before-sought-for freedom (for plastic bags have few aspirations), or maybe it was the westerly direction of the wind, when everyone knew weather never snuck in from the dry and lonely Kgalagadi. No one knew exactly what had caused it all, but everyone agreed that from the day the wind shifted, there was no way to go back to the way things had been before, because when the wind changed so did everything it touched.

Nono remembered the day well. She was at the till at Koppies and knew something was up when the number '1' button refused to be punched on the cash register. How could she ring up Mma Kgoroletso's considerable amount of groceries without the '1' button? And shouts and blood red faces from the manager, Mr Viljeon, were not going to help things.

When the wind shifted, the single working robot in the village decided to stop on yellow. It would have been much better had it stopped on red or even on green, but yellow was a problem. Yellow, an ambiguous colour, led to bang-ups and the inevitable fights, when each driver insisted that 'proceed with caution' meant he should proceed and the other guy should take caution. From that day, the four-way stop became a regular hang-out for the children from Khama Primary School down the road. They'd idle after school, forgetting all about the chores waiting for them at home, some of them were there for the crash-ups, others for the fights. All in all, quite a crowd turned out; so big, in fact, that Mma Moremi set up a table to sell magwinya and the yellow-aproned Quick Charge sellers added the four-way stop to their route around the village, charging people's cellphones.

That wind, for reasons no one ever did find out, brought all kinds of change and turbulence to the village. Winds can clear away litter or blow up the dust. They might pull up a loose roof so the sun can get a peek inside at the family secrets or knock down a tree and put an end to the family altogether. And sometimes, a stiff wind from the right direction, with the right suspension of pollen grains, dirt particles, and pollutants, can produce a heady mix that gives the brain a corrosive cleaning, waking up cells hidden inside lazy grey matter, cells that ignite thoughts that had been extinguished with the daily grind and boredom of life.

So it was for Tshepo. On that day of the shifted wind, when the '1' button stopped working on the cash register at Koppies and prices had to be rounded up to '2' or down to '0', when the robot stuck on yellow, providing a bit of entertainment for local school kids and a micro-economic boom for hawkers, and plastic bags were given dreams they never knew they had, Tshepo decided it was time to have an affair.

She'd never thought of having an affair before; it wasn't in her nature. She was a dependable Capricorn; at least that was what *Drum Magazine* told her. She was steadfast and trustworthy, and other such words that had no connection to anything as exciting as a love affair. She'd married Bruno after university, having known him since primary school. For her, life had always been a bit like knitting. The pattern was set; all you had to do was proceed: knit 1, pearl 1, knit 1, pearl 1. It wasn't difficult. You knew what came before and what would come after and there was not a whole lot of thinking involved. In fact, Tshepo thought, just like knitting, once you started thinking too much, once you started veering away from the pattern and improvising, things, almost without exception, went badly.

She and Bruno had been married a respectable twelve years. He was as predictable and dependable as her. A tough, solid block of a man with clear parameters of behaviour affixed firmly inside his skull making life an easy progression with few moral dilemmas. The two never had vicious arguments of which some couples regularly partook, nor the wild lovemaking that occurred after such events. They never threw dishes nor sped away in cars. They behaved civilly and had few disagreements. They had three equally unexcitable children who went to school, excelling at times or hovering on average at others, but never doing anything to warrant a visit to the school or the writing of desperate notes from teachers at the end of their tether. It was a simple knit 1, pearl 1 kind of life. Tshepo had always been happy with that.

With the shifting wind, though, Tshepo decided it would be a good idea to stuff the pattern in the drawer in the hall table and do a bit of making it up as she went along. She never thought for a minute about Bruno. Bruno had nothing to do with it. This affair was all about her. It was about expanding herself, about testing the waters away from the safety of the boat, seeing what it was like and if she could handle the waves. She had no intention of leaving Bruno. She loved him in a certain and kind way. She was sure she could develop a similar type of love with someone else, if she spent as much time with him as she had with Bruno, but what would be the point of that? Wastage was something Tshepo couldn't tolerate; she was all about efficiency. So, leaving Bruno was never going to be part of the plan. All Tshepo wanted was a brief excursion into the unknown, for the simple reason that she wanted to see what was there.

That decision made, next came the problem of implementation. How did one go about having an affair at the age of thirty-five? Where did one even start? Tshepo had trained as a teacher and had a lot of respect for the written word. When she'd been pregnant with her first child, she bought *Pregnancy for the First Timer* and *Those First Years*. When she and Bruno had wanted to build a house, she'd searched the library for architectural books until she'd stumbled upon *Ten Plans for the Perfect House*, and they'd built an exact replica of House No. 6, pages 231 through 237.

So, now that she needed information about how to have an affair, she, sensibly, set off for the library. To her surprise, there were a number of resources concerning how to set out on her new adventure. She started by searching under the topic of adultery, where she found many books and, later, magazine articles, written by spurned partners who explained at length how their devious other half had committed the offence. This gave Tshepo some ideas about how to proceed.

It seemed that the majority of affairs took place with co-workers. For Tshepo, this was problematic. At Bokamoso Primary School, where she taught standard six, all but three of the teachers were women. The first of the three to be struck immediately from consideration was the headmaster, Mr Olebogeng. Besides being her boss, which could lead to all types of problems, he was nearly sixty-five years old. The region had been begging him to retire for years. He had shrunk to the size of the average standard three student and couldn't hear unless the speaker shouted at gumba-gumba levels straight into his ear. Tshepo smiled when she thought about how proposing a love affair to him would require publicising it to half of the village at the same time. No, Mr Olebogeng was out.

The second one to be eliminated was the standard two teacher, Mr Didimala. Mr Didimala had a lisp. Tshepo had never thought she cared about his lisp. Others made silly comments in the staffroom, but she hadn't paid much attention to it. She was surprised that when it came to considering a person as someone with whom you might strip naked and jump into bed, a lisp took on a lot more significance. She thought a bit less of herself when she uncovered this hidden prejudice, but nevertheless, Mr Didimala was out.

The third candidate was more promising. Stone Maipelo was the groundsman. Ordinarily, Tshepo would have refrained from considering him. He had only a primary education and was at least ten years younger than her. She'd barely registered his presence before: he was just the boy who worked in the garden and gave her a 'Dumela Mma Nthebolang' every morning. But now that she was searching for someone to commit adultery with, Stone appeared to her in a different light.

He was tall and muscular with a fondness for American gangster clothes: big jeans dragging in the soil and falling to his hips and oversize T-shirts with pictures of people like Tupac or Che Guevara. In the new light, his walk was a deal clincher for Tshepo. It was a slow, rolling gait and, though she couldn't see under the big T-shirt, she suspected it pulled his hips into a smooth, rhythmic motion. Bruno walked straight and steady and if she was going to venture into this unknown territory she thought rolling hips might be the entryway.

Tshepo knew that for her plan to be successful, she'd need to proceed with some care. So, for just over a week, she slowly increased the amount of conversation she had with the young groundsman. 'Dumela Mma Nthebolang,' Stone said innocently on the Wednesday after, unbeknownst to him, he had won the position of Tshepo's partner in adultery.

'Dumela Stone,' Tshepo said.

Stone went back to his work of turning over the soil in the bed of geraniums at the front gate. He looked up with a questioning face when Tshepo remained standing in the same spot. 'Can I help you with something?'he asked.

Tshepo hadn't noticed the clear smoothness of his skin, and for a moment she was pulled off-track. 'Well ... yes, Stone. I was wondering what you put on those geraniums to get them looking so healthy?'

Though Stone dressed like an American gangster and rolled his hips when he walked, Tshepo discovered he spent most weekends at the gardening store and had twice won 'Best Houseplant' at the local agriculture show. As soon as Tshepo realised this, she knew the hook on which to dangle the bait. Each day when Tshepo arrived at school, she stopped for a few minutes at the gate to chat with Stone about flowers and soil and shade trees. In the evening, Tshepo read books about the same subjects so that she would appear to be what she said she was: an avid gardener.

So the days passed, until one morning, after a short discussion about the most recent accident at the yellow-stuck robot, Stone said, 'Mma Nthebolang, I mean, Tshepo' (she had insisted he use her first name) 'I thought you might like to come by my house after school knocks off. I have some new orange tea roses that I think you will really like.'

Tshepo smiled and said, 'Why Stone, yes, I would love that. 3:30 okay?'

It was agreed. 3:30 on a Tuesday afternoon in May, Tshepo would have sex with Stone. She said it in her mind, thinking that it would have some effect on her, a bit of niggling guilt at least, but nothing happened. She shrugged her shoulders, and went off to her classroom. The decision was made.

After school, Tshepo and Stone walked through the winding lanes of the village to his one-roomed house. Though his house was only cement blocks and corrugated iron, Stone had painted it pale yellow with red-trimmed windows and fascia board. It was a jolly little house and Tshepo was immediately put at ease. To add to the beauty of the compound, the garden was packed full of every plant imaginable. He had an orchard full of trees: pomegranates, oranges, peaches and morula. He had beds of flowers, some that spread out, some that grew tall and others that climbed a wooden trellis he'd constructed from old crates. He had cacti and aloes and bougainvillea in every colour. In the corner where he led her to see the tea roses, there was a little plastic table with four chairs where you could sit and admire the garden. There was something about the placement of the table and chairs that touched Tshepo. She reached her hand forward and ran it down the length of Stone's smooth cheek. 'This is so lovely.'

Stone looked at her, surprised, but didn't move. Her hand fell to her side and they stood in awkward silence for some minutes.

'Here are the roses,' he said, crashing through to the other side of the strange place they'd found themselves.

Tshepo looked, and then, fearful that her motives had not been apparent enough, said, 'Stone, I like you. What would you think about us making love?'

He obviously thought it was a good idea, because within a minute they were inside his house on the bed, struggling to remove their clothes. Tshepo was surprised by Stone's energy. Perhaps she had forgotten, but she couldn't recall Bruno ever being quite so energetic even in his younger years. It added a whole new, slightly manic aspect to the activity that Tshepo wasn't sure she disliked. His body was long and sleek, like a brown cat. He knew little about the biology of a woman apart from what he'd learnt in school, where clitorises don't exist and sex is described in the blandest of language; inserting tab A into slot B. Tshepo had to admit she had been right about the rolling hips, though.

When they were finished, which was in a surprisingly short time, Tshepo stood up and started dressing. 'Thank you for that, Stone,' she said once she had put her clothes back on and started out the door.

'So when will we see each other again?'

'At school, I guess,' Tshepo said, flattening her hair back into place in the bit of cracked mirror he had fixed to the wall.

'No, I mean *see* each other again,' Stone said, still lying naked on the bed.

'Oh no, that won't happen again. I'm married.'

Stone looked confused at first. 'Oh,' he said. After a few moments during which he appeared to be considering all sides of the situation, he continued, 'Okay.'

So Tshepo walked home to her house on the other side of the village. She wasn't feeling exactly as she'd expected, but she wasn't feeling bad either. She thought about Bruno and suddenly saw him in a very different way. Where Stone was all excitement and adrenaline, Bruno was a slow and steady builder, one who knew exactly where to put what to get the result he wanted. He had skills developed over the years that Tshepo hadn't ever recognised until now. Just as Tshepo had thought it would, her affair had opened up her mind a bit and let in some fresh air. Her life looked different through the eyes that had stepped out of it for a few hours. Her life had no airs nor falseness. No frantic excitement floating on bubbles, no foundation that needed constant repair. It was calm and loving, steady and true.

As she made her way through the winding lanes toward the centre of the village, she felt the wind that had blown constantly for two weeks slowly begin to fade, first to a light breeze then to stillness. Tshepo could hear her thoughts shifting in her head, making space for the adjustments brought about by the affair. When she reached the four-way stop, she found the robot had gone back to its cycle of green-yellow-red, green-yellow-red.

The children had straggled home to their long-awaited chores and Mma Moremi had gathered up the leftover fat cakes, thinking how she'd serve them to her husband and kids for dinner that night.

Tshepo walked through her front door and the home she knew so well looked changed. The sofas, which she'd always thought were a bit too hard, looked softer, and the colours in the painting above the fireplace, which had always gone unnoticed, looked sharper. Her daughter smiled up at her from the table where she worked on maths homework. Her son dropped macaroni into a boiling pot of water on the stove. They were hers, from her, of her. Bruno came through the door and found Tshepo standing in the middle of the kitchen, smiling.

'Are you all right, sweetheart?' he asked, kissing her on the cheek.

Tshepo smiled. 'I'm just perfect.'

The wind disappeared and things went back to normal – on the surface. Karabo Loeto, who had been at the front of the crowd watching the smashups, grew up to be an engineer who specialised in keeping robots running. Her friend, Michael Gababone, who'd watched the fights with a little bit more attention to detail than the others, moved to Las Vegas and became a professional boxing referee. Mma Moremi started Fat Cakes Galore with her profits she'd made during the time. Her specialty was magwinya stuffed with everything from sardines to whipped cream. Tshepo developed a love for gardening and held her steady Bruno and her average children a little closer to her heart.

At Koppies, they never did change the prices back to include '1'. It was only by accident, almost two years later, when Nono was varnishing her nails waiting for customers that she accidentally pushed the '1' button and realised that, after all of this time, it worked.

The Lies We Can't Hide

I WHISTLED as I climbed up the stairs to my small flat that day. I was happy, happier than I'd ever been before. I was marrying a wealthy, handsome man who adored me. I would never again experience the poverty and aching want of my childhood. I was entering the fairytale life I'd always dreamt of. That day, I should have slowed down a bit and savoured the simple raw taste of innocent happiness. I should have embraced it and held it close for just a little bit longer, because that sweltering December afternoon would be my last happy day for a long, long time.

I struggled momentarily at the door, fitting my key in the lock while carrying my packages: jewellery for the wedding, new lingerie and clothes for the honeymoon. Once inside, I dropped the bags at the door. The tiny flat was airless and roasting on that December day and I reached to turn on the fan in the corner. And it was then that something caught my eye. I shut the door behind me without taking my eyes from the table in the centre of the kitchen. There was something there, something that hadn't been there when I left.

I lived alone, and no one had been in my flat that day. If Thataone and I wanted to be together for the night, we always stayed at his house in Phakalane, he couldn't bear my 'tiny prison', as he called it. I moved toward the table cautiously and saw what it was. It was a knife.

Who had been here? Who could have left a knife on my kitchen table, and why?

For a moment, I panicked, maybe the person was still here! I needed to check the bathroom and the bedroom, the only other rooms in the flat. Maybe I should call someone, but they would all be at work on a Friday afternoon. So I continued toward the bedroom.

'Who's there?' I asked into the unknown. Both rooms were empty and the windows were closed. My flat had been locked, there was no way anyone could have got in without breaking a window.

I went back into the kitchen. I hesitated to pick up the knife, remembering police shows on TV where the detective would take the knife in for evidence, finger prints and DNA analysis. I laughed at myself and my wild imagination. It was just a knife. No one had been murdered. There was no crime committed and there would be no police. Someone had left the knife here, that was all. There were so many things on my mind, what with the preparations for the wedding, I could have easily forgotten someone leaving the knife in the flat.

I sat down on the Formica chair and took the knife in my hand. It was a three star knife, very common; many people had them. It had a brown handle with gold metal edging and three gold stars. It had once been broken and the end of the handle was held together with tightly wound black electrical tape. The blade, which could fold inside of the handle, was open. It was worn and had obviously been sharpened carefully to form a razor edge. I tried to fold the blade back inside, but because of the damage, it couldn't close completely. I rolled it around in my hand trying to think of where it could have come from. Many people had been in and out of the flat in the past few days. It could be anyone's. I was almost positive that it hadn't been there when I left. Nevertheless, I convinced myself that it had. I told myself that my eyes had let me down, that my mind was playing tricks, that I was tired from the wedding preparations and forgetful. I was still holding the knife in my hand when I heard my cellphone ringing in my bag, which was still lying with my packages at the front door.

I rushed to get it. 'Hello?'

It was Thataone. 'Are you still out shopping?' he asked. His deep, careful voice settled my mind.

'No, I'm home, I just got here.'

'You sound funny. Is something wrong?'

'No, not really. It's nothing, nothing at all.' I knew Thataone didn't like drama. He wanted calm, predictability. I'd got far by giving him what he wanted, and a forgotten knife would not mess that up now. 'It's just so hot. You know I don't have aircon in the flat, I'm melting.'

'Okay. Lefatshe, listen, my parents want to meet us tonight to discuss some last-minute details about the wedding. I'll come and collect you at seven. Is that okay?'

'Sure, I'll be waiting.'

'Okay, see you then. Love you.'

I closed the phone, picturing him sitting in his massive office on the top floor of the building his father owned. He was the head of legal affairs at Moremi and Sons, the only Batswana-owned diamond prospecting company in the country. They now owned three diamond mines in Botswana, one in Namibia and one in South Africa. Thataone Moremi was the eldest son of Matilda and Kgalalelo Moremi, their heir, and the most eligible bachelor in the country. I still wasn't sure how I, a poor girl from a no-name family in Serowe, had snagged him.

I had met Thataone at a fashion show at the Phakalane Golf Estate. Moremi and Sons was sponsoring the event and I was one of the fashion designers who had entered the competition. It was a very prestigious event and I had been nervous. My label was beginning to get some recognition, but there were big names at the event and I knew it would take a miracle for me to win. I was standing there, biting my fingernail and watching my first dress go out onto the walk.

'Be careful, you might bite your finger off,' I heard a voice behind me say.

I turned and saw him. I knew him, of course. Everybody did. He was beautiful up close. Tall, well-built, with light brown eyes, thin like a cat's, and a mouth always ready to break into a smile. He wore a loose shirt which I could see was pure silk. I wondered how such a fabric would feel against bare skin, and my own tingled at the thought. 'Are those yours?' he asked.

'Yes,' I said tentatively, not feeling able to withstand any negative comments at that moment.

'They're certainly unique,' he said, looking at the second outfit. It was a two-piece with a thin black strip of Lycra bound across the model's breasts and a long flowing vest in a rich purple velvet that met with a big black button strategically placed to keep the important parts at the front covered.

I turned to him and said, 'So you're a fashion critic too?'

He laughed. 'Hmmm. Feisty, I like that.'

Thinking back, I wondered sometimes about the ease of it all. You'd think finding your Prince Charming would involve a dangerous journey or a poisoned apple, but it was as simple as a few words passed between two people. That was eight months ago, and in two weeks' time we would be married. A Christmas wedding at Thataone's family's luxurious farm in the Tuli Block. I could hardly believe my luck.

I dropped the knife in my handbag, deciding I would ask my mother about it. It looked like something that she might have brought from Serowe, thinking she'd need it to chop vegetables or skin a goat at the wedding – despite the fact that I'd told her the preparations would be done by the army of workers at the farm, and that she'd be staying in an air-conditioned luxury chalet along with the other visitors, taking game drives and eating seven-course meals. That wasn't what my mother knew a wedding to be, and I could well imagine her holding tightly to her long-kept ideas and being sure a three star knife would come in handy despite what her daughter had to say.

The Moremi's house was magnificent. I knew I'd have to spend more than a lifetime in that house before I'd become blasé about it. There was a fountain in the foyer. A fountain in the foyer was probably enough to let a Mongwato girl from Serowe know that she was never going to be comfortable in that house.

'Oh, Lefatshe, don't you look as lovely as ever,' Mr Moremi grabbed my shoulders with his big meaty hands and kissed me once on both cheeks. 'Red certainly suits you.' He was a man of extremes. He was massive, with a stomach of awe-inspiring proportions. He spoke loudly. He drove big cars. Wore heavy gold and diamond encrusted jewellery. He had been a boy in tattered pants roaming in the bush surrounding Mochudi as a child. That boy of the bush was now one of the richest men in Southern Africa, number three in the last list that counted such things.

Mma Moremi was as opposite from her husband as a person could be. She was thin and small. Unless provoked, she preferred silence. She was abundant with nothing. Her movements were tight and curtailed. Her emotions were held close and given out in tiny packages which, much like the diamonds that had built her a house with a fountain, were held dear by those receiving them. I received one of her priceless gifts the first day I met her. She took me aside when we were at the car preparing to leave and said, 'For the first time Thataone has chosen with consideration.'

I kept that diamond shielded safely in my heart. When she came around the corner I smiled, genuinely happy to see her and to know that in a few days I would be her daughter-in-law.

'Lefatshe.' She hugged me for a moment against her slight body and whispered, 'I'm so happy, aren't you?' I nodded against her shoulder and felt tears build in my eyes.

'You're a bit late,' Mr Moremi boomed. 'Warona already has dinner waiting. We'll talk while we eat.'

It was a lovely dinner, both the food and the conversation. Thataone was quieter than usual, answering his parents' questions with mostly yes or no answers. He was always slightly tense with his father. Like most sons, he felt he didn't live up to what his father expected, but I never saw any sign of that. Mr Moremi was proud of his son, anyone could see that, except for Thataone. We stood at the door preparing to leave, and I took Thataone's hand in mine and he gave me a kiss on my cheek.

'It was a lovely evening Mr and Mrs Moremi, thank you,' I said.

'When will you start calling us Mom and Dad or at least Matilda and Kgalalelo?' Mr Moremi asked.

I smiled, embarrassed. 'Soon. I'm still getting used to things.'

Mr Moremi reached forward to give me a goodbye hug and accidentally knocked my purse off my shoulder. It fell to the floor, spilling the contents in a pile at his feet. 'Oh,

I'm sorry,' Mr Moremi said, and he and Thataone fell to their knees to pick up my things.

'What's this?' Thataone held up the knife. I'd completely forgotten about it. His eyes were wide as he held it.

'I … it's nothing. I found it this afternoon. I think it's my mother's. You know Mama. She probably brought it for the wedding.' I turned to his parents. 'She thinks she'll be doing the slaughtering.'

Mr Moremi got to his feet and handed me my handbag, but Thataone remained kneeling, holding the knife.

'Your mother? Your mother left this at the flat?' he asked from the floor.

'I don't know for sure. I just thought it must be her. It was lying on the kitchen table when I returned from shopping. Who else could have left it? Is it yours?'

Thataone stood up and shoved the knife in my handbag. 'Of course not. Mom, Dad, we need to go.' He went out the door and walked quickly to his car parked in the driveway. I said my goodbyes and followed him.

Inside the car I said, 'What's wrong? Is it the knife?'

He stared ahead. His hands gripped the leather of the steering wheel. He started the car and drove off. When he was away from the house, he pulled off the road and stopped. He turned to me.

'Where did you get that knife?' he snapped. 'Tell me the truth.'

I'd never seen him like that before. 'I told you the truth already. I came home from shopping and it was there on the table. I was surprised because I was sure that it hadn't been there before I left. But then I just thought maybe I hadn't seen it, or I'd forgotten somehow. I thought either my mother must have brought it, or my sister, Kenielwe. They're the only ones in the flat.'

'But that knife ... is it for me? Can it be?' he asked quietly, as if speaking to himself.

'How could it be for you? Thataone, please! You're scaring me. It's nothing. It's my mother's, it must be. I would never keep a knife like that. Do you think I meant to harm you?' I moved closer to him and put my arms around him. 'I'd never do that. I love you.'

I didn't want him like this. I didn't want anything like this. I wanted my handsome fiancé, my storybook wedding. His behaviour was so odd and out of place, out of character for the man I knew.

He started the car and drove me home in silence.

After the knife, Thataone changed. He was quieter and more cautious with me. I took it as wedding jitters and got on with things. I nearly forgot about the knife, though I found it hard to forget Thataone's reaction to it. He'd seemed almost frightened by it. Had he thought I was keeping a weapon to harm him? But why? I did everything I could to comfort him, to show him that I was who he saw, that there was no one hidden in the shadows waiting to pounce.

Around the time that the knife appeared, I began to have my baby dream. I'd always wanted children and I was sure that the dream was a premonition of our babies to come, Thataone's and mine. The dream baby was light skinned, fat and happy. He tottered around naked in my dreams. The dream was always the same. He would be walking toward me, smiling, happy, as he took the unstable steps of someone his age. Around his fat belly, he wore green traditional beads, dibaga, meant to keep him safe. Behind him I could see the hands of a woman held out toward the child as she let him go to walk to me. Just when he was about to reach me, the hands would fall away and I would wake up.

When I awoke from my baby dreams, though I knew them to represent happiness in the future, my future with Thataone's children, I always felt steeped in sadness. Though I wanted to concentrate on the baby, it was the hands that my mind's eye could not forget when I woke up. I wondered whose hands they were and why they disappeared when the baby finally made his way to me.

'Lefatshe? Are you there?'

'I'm here, Mama.' I rushed from the bathroom in a towel. 'I'm late, I know. Give me five minutes.'

'I'll make tea.' My mother moved toward the kitchen and I rushed back to the bedroom. We were leaving for the farm; the wedding was the next day and I was frantic with the details. I was fearful of forgetting things and had been packing and re-packing until I realised I was now late. I dressed and slammed the suitcase closed, carrying it out to the kitchen.

'Ready,' I said, smiling at my mother. 'And I could really do with that cup of tea.'

She set the cup in front of me and sat down. I felt better having her there. Her calm ways were just what I needed.

'What is this, ngwanake?' She held up a small leather bag. It was decorated with slices of ostrich egg-shells in the shape of a heart. It was the kind of craft-work done by Basarwa, but clearly this one had been made by someone with little skill, or perhaps even a child.

I took it in my hand. 'Where did you find this?'

'It was here. On the table. Is it some sort of lucky charm for the wedding?' she asked, smiling.

I took it in my hands. I could feel something in the small bag. I reached inside and pulled out a string of beads. They were the green beads from my dream, the ones the baby was wearing around his stomach as he made his way to me.

I threw the bag and beads on the table, screaming and moving away from them as if they had burnt my hands.

'Lefatshe, Lefatshe! What's wrong? What's happening?' My mother rushed to me and took me in her arms.

'Oh, Mama! What's happening to me? Who's doing this?'

After I calmed down, I explained about the beads and the knife. 'It could be anything, Lefatshe, anything at all. Maybe this bag is a good sign, a sign of luck. Luck for your wedding, your babies yet to be born.'

I was not convinced, but we needed to leave and I was getting married. No matter what, Thataone and I were getting married tomorrow. If there was nothing else I knew, if everything was confusing and not making sense, I knew that.

The road leading to the Tuli Block was lush and green. The rains had been good and the cattle were fat. Towering morula trees lined the road to the farm and troops of baboons squatted under them eating the fruit. I felt better once I was away from the flat. There would be an explanation for everything, but I didn't have time to find it now. I tried to push everything from my mind and think only of the wedding.

At the farm, guests had already arrived. Posh cars filled the parking area. Some people had already left to go game viewing, others were lounging near the pool. Thataone rushed up to the car when we arrived. He opened the car door.

'Hello, darling,' he said, giving me a kiss. 'MmaLefatshe, let me show you where you'll be staying.'

I watched them walk away and thought that what I needed now was a bit of time alone, to sort my head out. The long drive and the stress of the morning would fade away and I'd be ready to greet the guests. I'd been to the farm with Thataone a few times before, so I knew that there was a pretty path out near the workers' hostels that led down to the riverbank, and I headed off in that direction.

At the end of the line of hostels I came across Thataone's nanny, an old Mosarwa woman named Rakgadi 'Dumela Mma,' I greeted her.

She squinted at me through eyes blue with cataracts. She was old now, maybe in her late eighties or even her nineties, it was hard to tell. She was tiny, little more than bones rattling in her leathered, worn skin. She sat on a short stool, drinking from a chipped enamel cup something that smelt like traditional beer. 'O mang? Who's that?'

'It's me, Lefatshe, mosadi wa Thataone.'

She nodded slowly and patted the ground next to her. I sat down where she had instructed.

'You will marry tomorrow,' she started in a slow, cracked voice. 'I have known Thataone since the day he was born. He was always a greedy, selfish boy, but I love him anyway. I love him like he was my own.' She laughed quietly to herself, revealing the few teeth in her mouth.

Though I was tired and had thought I wanted to spend some time alone at the river's shady edge, sitting in the swept dirt of the old woman's compound seemed the only thing on earth that mattered. 'He grew up with my grand-daughter, N/qores, Land, just like you, Lefatshe, meaning the land, the earth. She was beautiful like a duiker. Do you remember?'

I hesitated. I feared that she was becoming confused as old people sometimes did. She was thinking that I knew this granddaughter she spoke of, but I didn't. I didn't want to be rude by pointing out her error, but I wanted to know more. 'No, no, Rakgadi, I don't know your granddaughter, I don't know N/qores.'

She smiled at her mistake. 'Oh yes, that's right. She was scared of you when you came. She hid in the house until you went back to the city.'

'Scared of me? Why? Where is she now?'

'She was in love with Thataone, just like you. She didn't want you to see. Love hung on her, no one could miss it and she feared you would see it and be angry.'

I became nervous. I didn't want to know any more, but I had to ask. 'N/qores and Thataone, they grew up together, they were friends?'

'Yes, Lefatshe, yes, ngwanake, they were friends. They loved each other. N/qores could not bear it anymore, the load she carried, and she walked away to the ancestors.' She sipped from her big cup.

'She's dead?' I asked.

'They say she is. We never found her, but it's three months now. She must be dead. She and her child.' The old woman looked down at her thin finger, where it drew circles in the sand.

'Her child? She was pregnant when she left?' I asked, though I didn't want to know. I didn't want to know anything else. I wanted her to stop talking, to refuse to answer any more of my questions. I felt sick.

'She was pregnant with Thataone's child. Of course, he was a rich Gaborone man, important and powerful. He could not marry a Mosarwa. N/qores knew that. We all knew that. He needs a wife like you. A beautiful Mongwato girl will suit him, make him happy. It is as it should be.'

I felt like I'd been hit in the stomach. My lungs were deflated and I struggled to take in air. What was happening? Why was this old woman telling me this? My ears were ringing so loudly that for a few moments her words were lost to me. Then the ringing stopped abruptly and I heard, '... all I have left is this, what N/qores made for me when she was a small girl.'

The old woman dug her gnarled hands inside of her ragged, faded dress. Hanging around her neck was the small leather bag decorated with ostrich egg-shells that I had found on the kitchen table at the flat. She held it out to me, the untidy heart just inches from my face. I stood and ran toward the house, wanting only to be far, far away from her.

That night I lay in bed, frightened by what was happening to me. I had told no one. I couldn't. I couldn't let go of my dream-life that easily. Why hadn't Thataone ever mentioned N/qores if she had been so important to him? Maybe he hadn't known she was pregnant when she disappeared. Still, why hadn't he at least mentioned her disappearance? It was wrong. And how had the bag with the beads come to be on my table? What did the knife mean?

My head was spinning and I fell into a fitful sleep. A noise reached deep into my dreams to pull me awake. The full moon showed through the window of my room when I sat up, wide awake. I waited for the sound. There it was. A baby. A baby was crying.

I got out of bed and opened the door. I could hear the crying coming from the bush behind the house. I went towards it, barefoot and in my nightgown, following the sound deep into the thorny bush. Although I stepped on sharp stones and thorns, I felt nothing. I needed to follow the cry. That was all that mattered.

The moon was high in the sky and I could see almost as well as if it were daylight in the bush. The crying was getting louder. I knew I was drawing closer. I pushed the branches of the sharp acacia trees to the side as I began to run. I came to a clearing in the brush, and there I could see a baby, lying in the middle of the opening, wrapped in a thin blanket, the moonlight caressing its tiny body.

I rushed toward it. When I came near, it turned to me. It was the baby of my dreams. He looked away, and when he turned back to face me a deep gash ran from his neck to his stomach, his guts spilt out of the wound and blood seeped into the soil around him. He cried out again, but when I reached forward to grab him, he disappeared.

I screamed and began to dig in the soil, thinking he had somehow fallen underground. I dug with my bare hands, pushing the soil between my kneeling legs. I dug and dug, crying out for the child. My hands began to bleed but I couldn't stop. I needed to find him before it was too late.

The topsoil had been hard and compacted, but once I got through the first layers, it became soft, as if it had been recently dug. Suddenly, I saw something, it was skin! I dug frantically. 'I'm coming!' I shouted.

I moved the soil away. What I saw put an end to any happiness I would ever know. It was not the baby I'd been searching for. It was N/qores, I knew it without question. She lay curled on her side, a wound from her neck to her stomach lay open, full of bugs and worms busy turning her back to the soil she had come from. Her hands caught my eye. Those familiar hands of my dream. Next to her lay the knife, the three star knife with the electrical tape on its handle. Thataone's knife, I knew it now. I understood everything now.

I can't say what happened after that. As the sun rose in the east and gave life to the bush around me, I, too, woke from a terrible nightmare. I sat on the ground next to a freshly covered hole. I was dirty, my feet and hands bleeding. My nightgown was torn and filthy. I knew what I had to do. I stood up and quickly made my way back to the house.

I slipped into my room without being noticed. My wedding dress hung from the edge of the wardrobe. Stripping off my nightgown, I stepped into the shower. I needed to wipe away all traces of my eventful night. I scrubbed with the soap until my skin was raw and watched the remnants of dried blood and red clay soil disappear down the drain. I stepped out of the shower refreshed.

It was a new day, Christmas Day, and I had to get ready for my wedding.

Jacob's New Bike

JACOB THOUGHT how funny it was that certain memories liked to force their way to the front of his mind. He was on his way to BeeBee Hardware when out of nowhere the Purple Lady popped up again. It wasn't that he didn't think about her often, because he did. The memory was worn smooth from rolling around in his mind for so long. He wondered why today, on his way to collect his new bike, the Purple Lady decided to push her way to the front.

The first time he'd seen her had been a long time ago, when he was just a boy in short pants and bare feet. His uncle had sent him to the semausu at the bus rank to buy tobacco. It was a drab day; the long dry winter had squeezed all of the colour out of the village, leaving only browns and greys behind. Even the bright red Coca Cola sign at the semausu was faded to a dull brick red, coated with dust churned up by passing buses.

Jacob bought the tobacco, but just as he turned to head back home something caught his eye. In the colourless landscape stood a bright vision. He stopped to take a closer look. He'd never seen such a beautiful woman in his life. She was dressed in a tie-dyed two-piece in a deep purple colour. The same material formed an elaborately tied scarf on her head, its ends fashioned into the wings of a bird at the front. She was tall, taller than anyone around her, and very fat. Her neck, where a thick gold necklace hung, had lovely rolls of fat that Jacob wished he could touch very lightly with the edge of his finger. Her skin was dark and smooth. Everything on her face was round; her eyes, her small nose, her thick round mouth and the deep dimples in both of her cheeks. Jacob couldn't take his eyes off her. She was like a purple iris growing in the barren Kgalagadi. Fresh and lovely.

'Get out of the road, you stupid boy!' the taxi man shouted and Jacob jumped to the side with fright. When he looked again, the Purple Woman was gone. Afterwards, he often wondered if she'd been there at all, or if she had simply got on the waiting bus and disappeared. From that day, Jacob knew what the image of a perfect female was and it had taken up permanent residence in his mind.

As he entered BeeBee Hardware with a smile on his face, checking the money in his pocket one last time with the tips of his fingers, the image of the Purple Woman filled his mind.

'My friend, I can see you are a happy man today. Today you will be riding your new bike away from my fine shop, no?' Hafiz, the Indian shop attendant, said to Jacob as he entered the store.

Jacob dug in his pocket for the P50 he had saved from his pay packet. 'Here you go.' Jacob handed the money to Hafiz. 'My last instalment.'

'I will go and get your bicycle.' And Hafiz disappeared into the dark storeroom at the back of the cramped dusty shop.

Over the years, Jacob had had his share of girlfriends, but he'd yet to find someone who could measure up to the Purple Woman. Nowadays, girls wanted to be like the models in the magazines, thin as a dog, with jeans hanging too low and shirts pushing up too high. Jacob kissed them and sometimes took them home to his one-roomed house, but they, like him, knew nothing serious would come of it. They could never marry a man who worked at the quarry, throwing stones into the big crusher, and who dreamt of owning a black Humber with a basket at the front and a carry rack at the back. They'd rather die than ride at the back of a bicycle. They were 'car girls', passing time with him as they waited for their motorised princes to arrive. Jacob wouldn't have wanted one of those silly girls on the back of his bike anyway. No, that seat was reserved for someone altogether different.

Hafiz came around the counter pushing the bike. 'Here it is, my friend!'

All Jacob wanted was to get on his new bike and ride and ride. He wanted to feel the wind blow his shirt back and forth with a flap. He wanted his muscles to ache from the strain of peddling. 'Thank you, Hafiz!' he called behind him as he left.

He pushed his bike carefully onto the road. Climbing on, he headed out to the edge of the village. It was Saturday, his day off, and he had made sure he had the entire day free to ride his new bike. He rode out past the fields of mealies, dodging herds of cows and stubborn donkeys. As the sun hit the top of the sky, he turned and headed back to the centre of town. He was hungry and looking forward to a chicken pie and a Coke from Monate Takeaway. As he waited in the queue, he glanced at his bicycle chained to a signpost outside, and thought how happy he was to have a bike that was strong and reliable, just as he'd wanted.

With his pie and drink, he sat down next to his bike on an iron bench outside the shop. It was a sunny day and since it was month-end, people were rushing back and forth, trying their best to use up all their pay. Just then, one of the big buses from Gaborone pulled up. Jacob watched without interest as the passengers, sweaty from the trip, climbed down from the bus.

He looked away for a moment, and when he turned back there she was

– the Purple Woman – though today she was wearing a complicated red and black Swazi pattern. Jacob shook his head, wondering if the sun was playing tricks on him. The Purple Woman would be an old lady by now, not a young, fit woman like the one before him. No, this could not be the original Purple Woman he decided, but she was almost an exact copy. Tall and fat and lovely, with the same smooth, dark skin and round, deep dimples.

Jacob left the unfinished pie and drink on the bench and, grabbing up his new bike, he ran toward the woman, pushing the bike along next to him. He would not let this one get away.

'Dumela Mma,' Jacob said when he was near her, but his voice was shaking and he couldn't be heard above the din of the bus rank. He tapped her lightly on the shoulder and tried again with more force. 'Dumela Mma,' he shouted in her ear.

'Ahhh!' she screamed, startled. But when she turned and saw Jacob she smiled and said in a soft, gentle voice, 'You don't need to shout.'

Up close, Jacob could smell her vanilla ice cream smell and he couldn't believe how lovely it was.

'Did you want something?' she asked, her round thick lips still curved into a smile bordered on each side by those irresistibly deep dimples. Jacob clasped the handlebars of the bike tightly to prevent himself from reaching out and touching them.

'I saw your packages … I thought maybe I could give you a lift … I have my bike.'

'On the back?' She looked him up and down. He was tall and thin, though his arms showed hard, tough muscles under the skin.

Jacob hesitated, his heart nearly falling on the melting tarmac of the road, wondering if in the end she was to be a car girl too. 'Yes, on the back,' he said softly.

She laughed, a tinkling that sent out sharp little bright bits that broke up the tense air between them and let in a welcome freshness from the heavens above. 'Okay.'

Jacob carefully stacked her packages in his big basket at the front and then steadied the bike as she positioned herself side saddle on the sturdy rack at the back. After a few false starts, he managed to get the bike going.

He could feel her ample weight at the back and he felt proud of his strong legs that could keep them moving. He knew that, given the chance, just his will and the finite matter of his determined body could design a happy, safe life for this woman. He pumped hard on the bike pedals and the wheels ran steady over the gravelled road. As they headed off, to where it was not yet decided, she grabbed his thin waist with her soft, plump hands and Jacob wished he could keep cycling and never stop again.

Complications of Closeness

I LOOKED out the open window in the small bathroom of my government house straight into the quivering heat. Though it was just past sunrise, the air was already weary, full of dust, burdened with the weight of the morning heat, and the day held a promise to get worse. The last time a drop of moisture had fallen from the sizzling sky had been more than twenty-seven months before.

I thought, as I watched a donkey pass through my front yard, of how there were children in New Xade that could walk and talk, but had never in their lifetimes felt the cool rain on their skin. They didn't know the dusty wet scent of the first tentative drops or the battering sound of it pelting the corrugated roof. They'd likely get a fright when the rain finally decided to fall, but until then we all waited as if holding our breaths. The tension built as the plants shrivelled, the animals melted down to bones covered by wind-hardened skin, the soil blew unabated, and the air cut sharp with each breath. I spotted a thin wisp of cloud hovering in the western sky, and though I knew that the sun as it crept higher would burn it off without effort, I thought, 'Perhaps it will rain today.'

I was still an optimist even after all of the efforts of this place to prove me wrong.

I had come to New Xade two years before to teach at the shiny new primary school the government had built to show the international troublemakers that they had only the best interests of the Basarwa, the bushmen, at heart. Despite two years of witnessing poverty with no exit, choices without sense, and prejudice at all corners, I, surprisingly, still had hope. I hoped that the Basarwa children I taught every day would break out of this place. I hoped that they would go on to become nurses and doctors, lawyers and law makers, to show other Batswana that they were equal, they were of worth. I had hope that these people, the people who ran the blood of humanity's first ancestors through their veins, would stand up and take their proper, proud role, instead of drowning yet another dispirited generation in a calabash of traditional beer. I had hope because of children like Cgara.

There had been Cgaras before her; Cgaras that broke my heart. Still when she arrived I could not stop myself from dreaming for her. I knew in my teacher's head that dreams could not be manufactured for someone else, but I also couldn't accept things the way they were. In other schools, schools on the eastern side of the country where most of the development was, in those schools, dreams filled up every classroom. They pushed and shoved each other to get to the front to be heard, to be realised.

The first time I entered my small classroom in New Xade, I was startled by the empty space. Not a single dream rushed to the front. Over those first few days, I searched the corners, under desks, behind the blackboard, but there was nothing. I tried to accept the situation, but the hollow silence was uncomfortable. I realised I couldn't teach in a classroom like that. I couldn't teach if there were no dreams for the newly acquired knowledge to attach itself to; so I started manufacturing dreams for my pupils.

At first, the dreams were few and they rattled around the classroom not sure of their purpose. But then I worked overtime. I packed them in, closing the windows and doors so they could not escape. I knew that they were not my students' dreams; I knew they were mine, but I pretended that was not the case.

After a while, I managed to delude myself into believing that at least some of the children who had once sat in Cgara's place in my heart had somehow taken a few of the dreams as their own. Once armed with their dream, they could then march forward and start the procession from this wind-swept, desiccated place. But each time, they would take a few bold steps, their heads held high and shoulders back, only to realise, once out the school gate, that the dream was not quite theirs. It would slip from their loose fingers and evaporate in the dry desert air. In that dreamless void, they lost courage. They succumbed to the ease of the path well worn, wandering down it in a dazed state, and I had to accept that I had failed with those ones.

But now there was Cgara. Cgara with the thin, fish-shaped eyes that flashed naughtily when excited. Cgara who had dreams that I hoped were finally hers.

As I was preparing my tea and toast that morning, I thought about how I could ask Cgara's parents if I might take her with me during the school holidays in December to my home village of Mahalapye, where my mother worked as a nurse. Cgara has said she dreamt of being a nurse one day. Maybe if she spent the month with my mother the dream would take a firmer hold.

I checked the clock; time to get going. I put my dishes in the sink and, just as I turned, I spotted a straw-coloured praying mantis sitting on the edge of the sink looking up at me, bemused. 'So what do you want?' I asked it.

I turned the tap on to allow a few drops of water to fall, thinking, in this drought, water would be the likely object of its search. It ignored the water and looked searchingly at me. I knew that some bushman tribes thought the praying mantis was a messenger, but I had no time to search for a diviner to tell me what this one had to say to me. I turned away from it and left for school.

The day began with a meeting in the staffroom, a place I usually tried to avoid. The other teachers at the school resented being sent to such a far-flung place, teaching children who wouldn't or couldn't pass. They thought the teaching service might forget they were there and they'd become part of the forgotten waste of the desert. Their black negativity banged against the windows of the staffroom and gave me an aching head. I sat near the window, opening it to let some fresh air in, hoping to dilute the putrid stuff that surrounded me.

Before the meeting started, a teacher I despised slightly more than the others, Mr Mogotsi, shouted across the room, 'So, Lapologang, did you hear that your pet is pregnant?' Chuckles radiated through the group and all heads turned to me. I looked up into his big, bulbous eyes sunk deep in the overhang of his forehead. His lips curled back, showing the pink inside, and I could see he was happy to be the deliverer of bad news. My stomach churned in disgust. 'Cgara, she's pregnant.' He smiled.

I sat quietly. I would not give him, or the others, the satisfaction of seeing me upset. I looked out the window at the parched air shaking in the relentless sun. I put my arm out to feel the hotness and the straw-coloured praying mantis landed on my upturned hand. Was it the same one? What did it want from me? Did it have a message about Cgara? Well, it was too late. I flicked it away in disgust.

I stumbled home after the meeting. I wanted to rest, to reorganise my brain. I lay on the bed and let the hot air from the window blow over me, and then I heard a small knock at the door. I got up and Cgara was standing in the open doorway.

'Madam, I know I'm not supposed to come here but I need to talk to you.' I pulled her inside, looking around to make sure no one had seen her, and closed the door behind us.

I sat down on the hard sofa provided by the school and Cgara sat on the Formica chair near the door. She looked down at her tiny hands resting in her lap. I noticed the praying mantis had returned, it sat on Cgara's shoulder. 'I don't want to disappoint you.'

I could feel my anger rising. 'Are you pregnant, Cgara?' I asked, not waiting for her to draw the courage to tell me on her own.

'Yes, Madam, I am.'

'How can you go to school and be a nurse with a baby? Why, Cgara? You're so bright.' I saw a flash and the praying mantis flew out the window.

Cgara just looked at me. I could see I was asking her questions for which she had no answers.

I knew Cgara's parents. They were in the group of Basarwa who had returned to the Central Kglagadi Game Reserve after the High Court ruled that they could. They lived a traditional hunter-gatherer life, relying on the land to take care of them. I wondered how they managed in this unrelenting drought. Normally, the headmaster of the school would need to contact Cgara's parents to let them know about her condition, but in this case he would have to wait until they turned up at the school. And that didn't happen until mid-November, when Cgara was already heavily pregnant.

I watched the group of dusty people walk up to the administration block. I thought that once they took Cgara away, I would probably never see her again. She'd strap her new baby on her back and join her family as they trekked through the desert on their daily quest for food. Dreams of making more of her life, dreams of being a nurse, would be lost. Hers along with mine.

'Those are my parents. I guess they've come for me,' Cgara said from behind my shoulder. I turned and saw the tiny girl. She looked like someone playing at being pregnant, as if she'd stuck a ball under her school uniform which pulled tight across her front. She was just a girl, it couldn't be true that she would soon be a mother. 'But don't worry, Madam, in this drought I'll not be a gone for long. I'll soon be back.'

I wondered what she meant. Would her mother take over the care of the child and allow Cgara to come back to school? That was common practice in the rest of the country, but school was not valued enough among the Basarwa to make allowance for that. 'So your mother has agreed to care for your baby?' I asked.

'No, she will kill it after it's born. If the rain doesn't fall, the baby must die. It's the best thing.' Cgara looked up at me with her clear eyes. It was shocking to hear her say it so simply, but I'd seen babies dying from hunger and knew how awful that could be. The desert was an unforgiving place, especially during the kind of drought we were having. People everywhere had ways to deal with their environment, who was I to judge?

I felt sick watching her trailing her parents away from the school. I wished she hadn't told me. For the first time in my life, I begged for ignorance, for some distance. Close up there are complex patterns crisscrossing and tangling with each other, making everything unclear. I couldn't pull my thoughts together. I had no idea where I stood on anything. I knew I was sad that Cgara was going.

I wasn't sure how I would feel when she returned, no longer pregnant, her child buried deep in the Kgalagadi. Shouldn't I feel happy that now she could get back on my dream-track toward her career as a nurse?

School closed and I planned to go home to my mother for the holidays, but I couldn't seem to leave. I watched the other teachers rush off, moments after the release bell, but I remained.

I sat in the cool air looking out at the navy blue of the evening sky. The straw-coloured praying mantis sat on the veranda wall looking up at me, occasionally snatching a nearby insect, holding it in its big claws and chewing away until the victim was no more. It had become my near-constant companion, but I no longer wondered what message it had for me. I knew. The problem now was what to do. Was I supposed to save Cgara's baby? But how? Was it even something I should be involved in?

I decided that I needed to get away from this place to get some perspective. I would leave tomorrow. I looked to where the mantis had been; it was gone.

I woke early the next day, packed my old Land Cruiser, and headed for home. I drove across the flat, barren land and thought of Cgara out there somewhere. What was she eating from that dry land? I passed the road going into the park. Without thinking, suddenly, I turned around. I couldn't just leave. Even if finding her would probably be impossible, I had to try. I couldn't live with myself if I didn't.

I drove into the park. Asking around, I managed to find a game ranger who told me where he had seen a group of Basarwa earlier that day. I followed his directions. Sheer luck brought me to them. It was Cgara's group. I could see her parents sitting in the stingy shade of a tattered acacia. I saw Cgara off to the side, her back to me. When I pulled up she turned. She was no longer pregnant. I stopped the car and jumped out, running toward her. 'Cgara! Where is the baby?'

Cgara looked up, confused. 'Madam, what are you doing here?'

'Where's your baby?'

'She didn't survive.'

I grabbed her by the shoulders. I shook her and shouted, screaming into her terrified face. I threw her to the ground violently. Her parents and a few dirty, thin adults and children with ring-wormed heads, pot bellies, and stick legs looked on, but remained silent. I turned to them, seething with anger. 'What have you done? Where is the baby?' Blank faces stared back.

Like a balloon deflating, my anger slipped away. I couldn't stay in a place where nothing made sense to me. I got in the car and sped away, fleeing, attempting to leave everything behind.

As I turned onto the tarred road, the first fat, dusty drops, the prelude to the storm building in the tall black clouds ahead, fell onto the windscreen. I picked up the praying mantis from the dashboard where it sat, eyeing me, I held it out the open window, and I set it free.

In the Spirit of McPhineas Lata

THIS TALE begins at the end; McPhineas Lata, the perennial bachelor who made a vocation of troubling married women, is dead. The air above Nokanyana village quivers with grief and rage and not a small amount of joy, because the troubling of married women, by its very definition, involved a lot of trouble. But, maybe because of his slippery personality, or an inordinate amount of blind luck, McPhineas Lata seemed to dodge the bulk of the trouble created by his behaviour, and left it for others to carry on his behalf. He had, after all, admitted to Bongo and Cliff, his left- and right-hand sidekicks, that troubling married women was a perfect pastime because it was 'all sweet and no sweat'.

Women in the village of Nokanyana, named after a small river that no one had yet been able to discover, were notoriously greedy, and, without exception, surly. Husbands in the village were all small and thin with tight muscles worked into knots because they spent all of their lives either working to please their wives or withstanding barrages of insults and criticisms for failing to do it up to the very high expectation of Nokanyana women. For Nokanyana men, it was a lose-lose situation and, as a result, each and every one of them despised McPhineas

Lata merely for remaining single – he had made the right decision and they had not.

McPhineas Lata, though thus despised by most husbands, was adored by most wives. His funeral was full of dramatic fainting and howls of grief echoing as far as the Ditlhako Hills. Tears fell by the bucketful and nearly succeeded in creating the village's missing namesake. The husbands stood at the back of the gathering wearing variations on the theme 'stern face' while the minister said his last words. When it was time to pour dirt on the coffin of McPhineas Lata, the husbands rushed past their crying wives and grabbed up the shovels. Some even came prepared with their own to make the work faster. Indeed, no one could remember a burial that had lasted for so short a time. No sooner had the wives heard that first shovelful of soil hit against the wooden coffin, as they were still organising themselves for their final grand crescendo of wailing, than the soil was seen to be heaped into a great mound over the grave. The men then piled stones on top, of a great number sure to keep McPhineas Lata firmly in his eternal bed. The men stacked the shovels by the grave, slapped the soil off their hands, and led the way back to the village, leaving all their McPhineas Lata problems in the cemetery for good. Or so they thought.

As the husbands made their happy ways to Ema Rengwe Bar, MmaTebogo, one of McPhineas's greatest fans, lingered behind, looking longingly at McPhineas Lata's grave. She wondered how the women of Nokanyana would manage without such a talented man. She also wondered what the women would do with all of their spare time. There was only so much husband-haranguing a woman could stand. She thought about how much she personally would miss McPhineas Lata and, without so much as a warning, her mind floated away into McPhineas Lata Land.

Naledi Huelela stopped on the thin lane leading from the cemetery to the village and looked back at McPhineas Lata's grave and spotted MmaTebogo. 'What does she think she's doing?' she asked with indignation. The wives stopped and turned to see MmaTebogo lying on top of McPhineas Lata's grave. 'She can't do that!' Naledi said. She felt quite proprietorial over McPhineas Lata since he had died in her bed in the middle of one of his more gymnastically performed sessions. It really had been quite extraordinary what he could get up to. People said he read books.

'Read books?' Bongo responded with a sceptical air when asked by the husbands who had gathered at Ema Rengwe Bar after the funeral.

Though they had left the cemetery in a jovial and confident mood, a comment by Zero Maranyane put paid to that. He had looked up from his first beer and said, 'I doubt our wives will forget him as quickly as we will.'

It was a bitter taste of what their McPhineas Lata-less future was going to hold. No, Nokanyana wives would not forget McPhineas Lata. It would have been better if he had lived to a ripe old age, when his muscles and frail, old man body would have let the wives down and would have had them drifting back to their hard-done-by husbands.

Instead, he died as virile as ever; for god's sake, he died in the act of one of his more acrobatic performances, or so the husbands had heard.

The husbands were in a predicament. They knew enough to realise that a dead and buried McPhineas Lata didn't mean dead and buried McPhineas Lata memories. Memories that would likely swirl and twirl in their wives' minds, adding salt and strength until McPhineas Lata became an untouchable super-sex hero with whom they could never compare. They realised then that they had quite a problem with McPhineas Lata dead and buried. Their wives had been almost manageable when he was around, but now the husbands expected the worst.

So they grilled McPhineas Lata's left-hand sidekick, Bongo. 'McPhineas Lata reading books? No, he was far too lazy for that. Mostly, I always put it down to a good imagination,' Bongo offered. 'Imagination?' the husbands asked. If that was the case, they were most certainly doomed.

RraTebogo stood up to address the husbands. He was in the same rudderless boat as they were, but he knew they needed a plan if there was to be any hope at all. 'Men! Men! If McPhineas Lata had imagination, why can't we get some of it? Why not? Just because we never had imagination before, doesn't mean we can't change. To be honest, I don't think we have a chance if we don't.' Then he turned to McPhineas Lata's right-hand sidekick, Cliff. 'So did he ever give you any pointers? Any advice?'

Cliff, not the brightest bulb in the box, looked to Bongo for help. 'He did say once that it was good to regulate speed,' Cliff offered up as assistance. The crowd nodded in approval.

Some took out pocket-sized notebooks and wrote down the advice, but before they put a full stop on the sentence, Bongo added, 'But he said speed was also dependent on the woman's likes and dislikes.' The crowd's elation at their perceived progress fell like a lead balloon when they found they were back to the start line.

A particularly gnarled and knotty fellow named Tobias Oitlhobogile stood up. Hunched over, he said in a battered voice, 'Maybe we should work together to come up with McPhineas Lata's method. I don't see any of us finding it out on our own.' The husbands nodded. It was better that way – at least if they failed, which in all likelihood would be the outcome, together it wouldn't feel so personal. And they could always meet at Ema Rengwe to commiserate; at least that would be something to look forward to.

So while the wives were fighting it out, trying to climb on top of McPhineas Lata's rocky grave to give him a few last humps, the husbands made a plan of how together they would, by the process of elimination, come up with McPhineas Lata's secret for satisfying their wives.

RraTebogo, the headmaster at the local primary school, rushed to collect a blackboard which he and Ntatemogolo Moeng carried back to the bar. They would use it to map out their plan. They knew that there were only so many things that one could do when it came to making love so they divided the work into a few main categories. The husbands had decided to work in a logical, deductive manner. They would start broadly and work down to the intricate details. All evidence collected would be brought back to Ema Rengwe, discussed, and compiled into notes by the elected secretary, Mr Mokwadi Okwadile, the local accountant. They were going to be systematic and with a good effort by everyone, they were almost assured of success.

The women trickled home from the cemetery over the next week, tired and hungry and more surly than usual. A thunderstorm on the weekend meant no woman could buck and ride on the grave as she mourned McPhineas Lata, and the men knew the time had come to begin collecting the information they needed.

RraTebogo was given the broad topic of foreplay. Once Tebogo, their son, was born almost thirty-six years previously, RraTebogo had thought, as was the natural course of things, that foreplay should be abandoned in lieu of sleep. Reintroducing such a long-forgotten activity after such a substantial period of time proved to be a bit touch and go. On his first attempt, which even he recognised later as slightly overambitious, MmaTebogo stuck her head under the covers and responded, 'What the hell do you think you're doing, old man?' Lost for words, RraTebogo rolled over and went to sleep.

The next day he decided he'd have to take things a little slower. Before getting down to business, he rubbed her right shoulder for three minutes. The time-span he knew for certain as he made sure the digital alarm clock Tebogo had bought them for Christmas was positioned at the correct angle so as to be seen from the bed. Then he stroked her left side four times in sequence and promptly proceeded with the business. Since MmaTebogo neither shouted nor hit him, he marked it up as a success and passed his news on to the others that night at Ema Rengwe.

Mokwadi looked up from his notebook, his eyes swimming behind his thick, Coke-bottle glasses. 'Was that four minutes on the shoulder and three strokes on the side?'

'No,' RraTebogo corrected him. 'Three minutes on the right shoulder and four strokes on the left side. Don't forget that left. I might be a bit subjective, but it seemed that the left side is the right side for the stroking. Anyway, we'll know soon enough.'

And indeed they would, for once something was seen to work all of the husbands took the bit of information home and put it into practice in their beds. So for a week of nightly sessions in each and every home in Nokanyana, husbands were giving their wives three-minute rubs on the right shoulder and four strokes on the left side before getting down to the business. The wives were curiously quiet throughout the week. A few hard-cores still climbed up the hill to the cemetery to cavort with the memory of McPhineas Lata, but the rest stayed at home, more confused than anything. Something strange was happening in Nokanyana and they didn't want to be up on top of McPhineas Lata's grave and miss the uncovering of all this mysterious activity.

Back at Ema Rengwe the husbands were in a jubilant mood. Things were going well with the foreplay. 'It is time to move on!' RraTebogo said, bringing out the heavy blackboard from the bar storeroom. 'Okay, Ntatemogolo Moeng. You've been assigned breasts, any progress there?'

The husbands' eyes moved to the old man sitting on a stool in the corner. He stood up straight and repositioned his jacket, circa 1972, evidenced by the massive lapels and 4 cm by 4 cm checked pattern, red on tan. 'Thank you, Modulasetilo. I am happy to report that I have nothing at all to report.' The old man bowed slightly and repositioned himself with no small amount of effort on the tall stool.

'Well, have you tried anything?' RraTebogo asked in desperation. 'Even a negative result is helpful.' The husbands nodded their heads. They all knew that a hard smack from a big, disagreeable wife would teach them a lesson they wouldn't soon forget.

Ntatemogolo Moeng stood up again. 'Thank you, Modulasetilo. Yes, I have tried a few things but they seem to have just made Mma Moeng very annoyed. She has taken to bringing a softball bat to bed, so considering my age and the fragility of my bones, I thought it best to stop along the way. It was a matter of health.' He climbed back up on the stool.

RraTebogo was annoyed. 'Bloody hell, man, just tell us what you did so we can all avoid it. I don't think any of us cherish the idea of getting hit in the head with a bat!'

'Thank you, Modulasetilo. I can say that it appears squeezing of breasts is a bit tricky – considering all of the patterns and rhythms and varying levels of pressure – I really didn't know where to start. And then, I know some of you more ambitious young men might even include some mouth activity. I just didn't know where to start, honestly, so I thought since the two milk cows in my kraal seemed to accept the pattern I used on them, I started there. Sort of a milking action. But as I said, MmaMoeng didn't take kindly to that.'As he climbed back up onto the high stool, the husbands let out a collective groan and shook their heads.

RraTebogo tried to be respectful of the old man's age. 'Are you saying you were milking your wife?'

Ntatemogolo struggled down off the stool and stood, though slightly bent from all of the effort. 'Yes, Modulasetilo, that is exactly what I'm saying, but be warned, I wouldn't advise it.' He climbed back up onto the stool with a sigh.

RraTebogo looked at Mokwadi. 'Did you write that down? We certainly don't want to go that route again.' He turned to the husbands. 'Does anybody have anything to report? Anything at all?' He couldn't help but sound discouraged. He knew a few shoulder squeezes and side strokes were not going to push the legend of McPhineas Lata out of the wives' minds. 'I have noticed a few of our wives have taken to drifting back to the grave in the late afternoon. We husbands are losing ground!'

RraTebogo looked around and saw nothing but a crowd of disappointed faces. 'Come on, men, we need to put in more effort.' Then, hesitantly, the secretary raised his hand. 'Yes, Mokwadi, do you have something for us?'

'I'm not quite sure. As you know, I was given speed as my area, but I discovered something that has nothing to do with that. I don't know if it is in order to mention it or not.'

'Give it over, man! Can't you see we're desperate here?'

'Well, I was experimenting with quite a fast speed and MmaMokwadi shifted to get a better view of the TV and I slipped off her and fell to the side. I happened to settle right next to her and since I was slightly out of breath, being not used to such high-energy activity, I was breathing hard right in her ear. Suddenly she picked up the remote and shut off the TV. As the week progressed, I added a few licks of my tongue and kisses on her neck and I believe I'm on to something.'

The Nokanyana husbands burst into cheers. Some rushed forward and slapped the shy accountant on the back.

RraTebogo stood up to get some order. 'Okay, okay. This is only going to work if we can reproduce the moves in our own homes. Mokwadi, show us on the blackboard.' The slight man stood up and took the chalk. He quickly drew a diagram complete with arrows and times to show how the husbands should approach this new move. The house agreed it should be inserted in the routine after the shoulder rubbing and the side-stroking, and before the business. That night the Nokanyana husbands went home a happy lot. They began to believe that they actually could replicate McPhineas Lata's moves and that their wives would forget all about that dead wife-troubler.

MmaTebogo was at the communal tap filling her water tank when Patience Okwadile pushed up with her wheelbarrow loaded with two large buckets. They greeted each other and sat quietly together; Patience on the edge of the wheelbarrow, MmaTebogo on an upturned cement block, both nibbling at the words they wanted to say while watching the thin stream of water fall from tap to tank. 'Too bad about McPhineas Lata,' MmaTebogo started, hoping that Patience would pick it up and lead them to the topic filling both of their minds.

Patience adjusted the purple and red doek on her head, and then glanced at MmaTebogo from the corner of her eye. 'Everything fine there at home?' she asked.

'Yes,' MmaTebogo answered. 'Why do you ask?'

'Nothing unusual?' Patience wanted a bit more before she let her tongue wag freely.

'Well, now that you mention it.' And MmaTebogo began explaining the changes taking place in her matrimonial bed.

Patience listened but, like most people, she listened through ears that filtered things to be skewed in a general direction already decided by her. When MmaTebogo finished, she asked, 'So is it three minutes on the right shoulder and four strokes on the left side?'

MmaTebogo's eyes widened. 'Yes! Yes! That is exactly it! Every night like clockwork. Then there are a few minutes of blowing in my ear, five to seven kisses on the neck, and then the business.'

'Aha! I knew it!' Patience said, jumping to her feet. She now had enough evidence to confirm what she already believed. She told MmaTebogo her theory. 'He's here … with us. I knew he couldn't just leave like that. McPhineas Lata has taken up the bodies of our husbands. He has taken spiritual possession of the husbands of Nokanyana.'

MmaTebogo, a practical woman, said, 'Do you think so? Can that even happen?'

'Sure, why not? What else could it be?'

MmaTebogo had to agree that she had no answer to that question. Maybe Patience was right. The two decided to call the wives to see if in their bedrooms they were experiencing the same transformation.

'It starts with three minutes on the left shoulder,' Karabo John said the next morning, at the meeting at the church at the end of the village.

'Left? Now that's an interesting twist,' MmaTebogo commented.

'Why would McPhineas Lata change things for only one of the wives?' The wives nodded their heads in agreement. It was indeed unusual. Maybe the theory was not correct after all.

But then Karabo John remembered, 'Okay, no ... you know Dimpho has a problem, he never could keep left and right straight.'

The wives giggled. That was the answer then. It was true, they decided, McPhineas Lata had not left them when he died, he had only taken up residence in each of their husbands' bodies. They were so relieved. Many had wondered how they would go on without their weekly visits with McPhineas Lata and the grave humping was just not cutting it.

'Now it's even better,' Naledi Huelela added. 'Now we all get McPhineas Lata – every night. No more sharing!'

'He really is a wise man,' MmaTebogo said, nodding thoughtfully.

As the sun set in Nokanyana, husbands and wives had big, wide smiles planted firmly on their faces and deep in their hearts. Once darkness descended, they hurried off to their bedrooms, leaving children to fend for themselves; favourite television dramas were abandoned in the rush, as husbands and wives could hardly wait to discover what new between-the-sheets tricks and treats McPhineas Lata had in store for them.

A Memory of Mother

THERE WAS a memory, faded on the edges, which she kept folded and held in the side pocket of her heart. It was of sitting on a mat of grass by a river under the protective shade of a giant pepper tree. Her mother was laughing, leaning back, her elegant neck exposed, her perfect calf kicked skyward. The man sat next to her, trapped in a gaze of needy amazement, eyes fixated by her mother's beauty. A baby, baby Nono, lay asleep on the patchwork quilt, slightly away from them, her thick lashes resting on her innocent cheeks. And she sat next to Nono, guarding her as always, chasing flies from her fat, brown face. Her legs stretched straight in front of her, her cotton dress tucked tidily under them, her hands resting, palms down, on her thighs waiting to be needed. A good girl. Karabo, always the good girl.

She liked that memory, though she wasn't sure she trusted it. Where that river was, she didn't know, and this made her question almost everything else about the memory – though not too vigorously. It was the only one she had, and holding on to it helped her to believe that the story of her mother was something more than a myth to make her sleep on a stormy night. She held her mother secure in that frayed, unsure memory.

She had it folded away tightly that evening. Her mind was elsewhere. Gran was sick and Nono needed new school shoes, and her mind couldn't stay attached to the maths she needed to finish before the candle melted away in its holder. She was startled when a hard knock rattled the loose door. She stood and pushed the faded curtain aside to see who was pounding like a policeman in the night when people should be home letting the day wind out its last hours in peace.

It was a woman. It took only a quick scan of her thoughts, a peek at the folded memory and Karabo knew – it was her. After nine years, her mother was standing on the other side of their door.

'Who is it?' Gran shouted from the one and only bedroom. Karabo ignored her grandmother's question. She stood holding the table with shaking hands, waiting for her thoughts to calm and her stomach to settle.

She feared the real mother waiting on the stoop. She preferred the one in her memory. That one was happy and kind and loving. She was a mother who brushed out her daughters' hair and fixed it with shiny coloured ribbons. One that sang songs with them, and was proud of her daughters' small achievements.

A mother who cried with them when they failed. She was a mother who didn't walk to the shop for cigarettes and never come back again.

Once Karabo opened that door, the mother who'd lain in the cool shade with the sound of the flowing river in the background would vanish, never to be conjured up again, leaving only the mother made of blood and bones and mistakes and pain. The mother she didn't want, who had nothing to do with the folded memory in her heart pocket.

But Karabo, always the good girl, took the key from the nearby hook and opened the door to the stranger standing there, and felt the slight tickle of her memory, held dear for so long, slowly slip away into the cool night air.

The Rich People's School

SYLVIA MOVED to the huge granite boulder, now warm from the early morning sun. It was a ritual when she was here, especially on the cold days. The boulder would catch the sun until it was teatime at school, and when the sun moved completely off the boulder, she would move slowly down the dry riverbed making her way back to the corner at the end of the road near the school where she would wait for Gran.

She would have preferred to stay at home all day, and not sit here at the river. She liked being at home, just her and Gran. She liked following her around, Gran carrying the big metal watering can and she the small plastic one, watering the spinach in their tidy plots. Sylvia liked watching the water seep into the thirsty ground. She liked sweeping the yard with the broom made of grass until it lay tidy with engraved swirl patterns across its surface. But Sylvia knew that it would cause trouble if she refused to go to school, so instead she spent each morning on her warm river boulder.

A blue-headed lizard climbed very near to her bare leg sticking out from under her neatly ironed uniform. It didn't even know she was there; thinking her leg another part of the stone, it too was searching for warmth. It nodded its head as if in greeting, though only in her mind, because not even a lizard would greet a stone. Sylvia wondered sadly, then who would? Unthinkingly, she rubbed the stone in commiseration and the lizard dashed away in fear.

Lying back, Sylvia gently fell asleep. Her mind took her to her mother. Not in distance, not far away in America where she lived with her new family. Her mind carried her to her mother in time. To before school, when she was small and her mother lived with them at Gran's. They were all happy then.

But then her mother had met the American. There was no way he could live in a dry, backward desert, he had said in his big voice that vibrated the walls of their small hut. This was no life for him. If Sylvia's mother loved him, she would come back with him to his home in America. 'But what about Sylvia?' she had asked. No, Sylvia could stay with Gran, she won't mind, it will be better for her.

Then she and Gran were alone. There was food, because money came every month from America to be collected at the Western Union counter at the post office, jealous eyes watching and nasty tongues talking when Gran and Sylvia left. Sylvia's mother had agreed to leave her behind only if the American agreed to pay for her to go to the rich people's school, the one on the hill where every student grew up to become a doctor or a lawyer. And so he did.

Sylvia recalled the day her mother left. The car stood running, the American waiting inside, every minute or two calling out the open window, 'We'll be late! We'll miss our plane!' Sylvia's mother stooped down next to Sylvia in the well-swept dirt of the lolwapa even though she wore the expensive white suit the American had bought her. 'I will come and see you one day and you will be a big, clever, girl. You will go to university and have so many choices and not have to sell your life away like your silly, stupid mother.'

Sylvia remembered the tears falling from her mother's beautiful eyes, and the long, low moaning sound Gran made deep in the night while she thought Sylvia lay asleep next to her.

They managed though, Sylvia and Gran. Sylvia hardly noticed how their sadness hid behind the tasks of living.

Then the time came for Sylvia to go to the rich people's school. On a hot summer morning she set off with Gran who carried a thick roll of money in her dress pocket.

When Sylvia saw the school she thought perhaps she had been taken to another country. Smooth, grass-covered lawns were being watered from hidden pipes in the ground. Flowerbeds bloomed in every rainbow colour. Children laughed and chased each other around brightly painted jungle gyms and swings. Sylvia had never seen a school like this. She only knew the government school near their home, with its wide, dusty yard scattered with broken desks.

She smiled at Gran, but Gran looked back at her with a face Sylvia had never seen before. It was a face of anger and fear at the same time. Sylvia wondered if Gran was afraid of the water shooting from the ground or maybe she was worried for the children swinging so high on the swings. 'You must behave now, do you hear?' she said in someone else's voice.

'Yes, Mme,' Sylvia said, wondering how Gran could be frightened and angry when everything looked so lovely.

They walked up the shiny, polished red steps of the brick building. A thin white woman sat at the desk. She spoke in English to Gran, and Gran spoke back, looking down at the floor the whole time. She handed the woman the big roll of money and the woman wrote something on a piece of paper and handed it to Gran.

When they went out the door, back to the shiny steps, Sylvia was surprised to see that a small group of children had gathered. They stared at her and Gran as they walked down the path and out the front gate.

In the morning, Gran woke Sylvia before the sun rose and washed her in the big zinc bathtub outside. Then she brought out Sylvia's brand new school uniform and shiny black school shoes. 'You look smart, Sylvia. Very smart,' Gran said, turning her around to see all sides and smiling.

Before reaching the school, Gran stopped. 'It's better I leave you here, Sylvia. There's the gate, can you see it?' Sylvia nodded. 'You go in that gate and ask for the standard one class. They will take you there, just tell them your name. Be a good girl. I will be right here when you finish.'

Sylvia looked at Gran and wondered why she was behaving so oddly. Perhaps she was sad that all day she would be at home alone without Sylvia to talk to.

That was many weeks ago now. She had found her classroom. Inside was a tall Indian teacher at the front who spoke in English, tilting her head from side to side and smiling, showing her white teeth all of the time. The children in Sylvia's class were small like her, but she knew none of them. Some were black, some were brown and some were white. Sylvia had never seen white children before and spent much of the morning sneaking shy looks at them.

When teatime came, Sylvia followed the other children to the tables under the shades near the playground. She opened the plastic container that Gran had packed in her new school bag. Inside was the left-over pap and spinach from the night before. Her stomach growled when she saw it and she began eating straightaway, not noticing that children were gathering around her.

A girl with long braids from the hair salon plaited into her hair said, 'Look at what she eats!'

Children stood with their tinned sodas and chips in packets from the shops and laughed. Sylvia, not knowing enough English, understood nothing of what they were saying, but became scared as they gathered around her, more and more of them. She stopped eating and looked down at the table hoping that they would leave her alone. Suddenly a boy rushed forward and grabbed her container, the one Gran had bought new for school, and ran away with it, throwing the pap and spinach on the green lawn along the way. Sylvia tried to catch him but he was big and fast. She shouted, 'Stop!' but he didn't. A bell rang and the boy dropped the container and stamped hard on it, smiling all of the while. When he ran past Sylvia, he said, 'Go home, poor girl!'

Sylvia picked up the pieces of the container and walked out of the school gate. She waited at the end of the road until Gran arrived. She lied to Gran, telling her that the teacher said that they mustn't bring food to school any more, that the container would stay there and the teacher would fill it with food instead. 'That's very kind of them,' Gran said, relieved that all had gone well. And Sylvia smiled up at her, agreeing.

That was Sylvia's last day at the rich people's school. Still, every morning Gran would drop her at the end of the road and pick her up every afternoon at the same place. Sylvia would be full of all the stories about school and her friends there. At night around the fire where they cooked, Gran would talk about how one day Sylvia would be clever and rich and they would fly together in an aeroplane to see Sylvia's mother.

'Your mother did the right thing, Sylvia. You shouldn't think she didn't. We will go and fetch her when you are rich from learning everything at the rich people's school.' Gran would smile and take Sylvia into her soft jellied arms and hold her tight. Sylvia would be almost happy, save for the part of her that knew lying was wrong and that now maybe because she wasn't going to the rich people's school they would never get her mother back.

Sylvia woke up from her dream, looked at the sun and realised that she was late. Climbing down from the boulder, she tried hard to walk quickly along the riverbed but the sand kept swallowing her footsteps. By the time she reached the corner where Gran should have been waiting, she could feel small streams of sweat running down her back.

Where was Gran? Looking in the direction of the school she could see that it was even later than she had thought, the rich children had all been taken home in their parents' cars. Everything was very quiet.

Sylvia panicked. How would she get home? She didn't know the way well enough through the thin winding lanes in the village. Just as tears began to fall down her face, she saw Gran coming towards her from the direction of the school. When she saw Sylvia she began to run.

'Where have you been? I thought now they have taken you too and I would be an old woman all alone,' she said, grabbing up Sylvia in her arms, holding her tight until Sylvia thought she wouldn't breathe another breath. Then Gran set her firmly on the ground, holding her out and putting an angry face on hers where it didn't belong. 'Why have you not been going to the rich people's school?'

Sylvia didn't know what to say. She didn't want Gran to cry when she found out that they might never be able to go and fetch Sylvia's mother in America just because she was frightened of the rich children. 'I don't like it there,' she said in a soft voice.

Gran pulled the big roll of money from her coat pocket and held it out for Sylvia to see. 'Never mind. You'll go to school near our house. Maybe you'll be a teacher, they are rich too, Sylvia. Do you know that?' Sylvia nodded. 'We will not tell your mother. When the school money is enough, we will send it back to her and she will come home to us.'

She smiled down at Sylvia and Sylvia smiled up at her wise and clever Gran, who took Sylvia's small hand in hers and they walked home.

Her Husband's Hands

SHE TURNED to let the wind blow a wayward hair out of her face and there he was standing, tall and still. Not even the dogs lying in the cool shade of the morula tree had barked to give warning. Looking up at the man from where she knelt in the patch of spinach she'd been weeding, she asked him a bit too sharply because of being startled, 'What do you want?'

The late morning sun was behind him so his features were in the dark. His head was long and thin, his clothes tidy but dated. He was still, as if his blood stopped in his veins, so still that even the wind did not blow his shirt sleeve or the leg of his trousers. It was as if he stopped the invisible particles of the air from moving around him with the solid force of his self. 'I'm looking for work,' he said.

She reached for her walking stick and struggled to her feet. 'We need people to bring in the melons for the next couple of weeks, then the butternuts will come ripe. How much time have you got?' she asked him.

'As much as you need.'

Ten years ago to the day, her husband went out to the fields to check the maize before sunrise, and just as his breakfast was cooling on the table, Boss-boy came flying through the door. 'MmaKenny, RraMoleele's passed out in the field!' When she got there, he'd already been dead for more than an hour.

Years had passed, but the ache in her chest whenever she thought about that day had not lessened. Her son, Kenny, wanted her to move to Gaborone and live with his family, but she couldn't walk away from her husband's memories imprinted on every block of the house he'd built, the trees he'd planted, the bed he'd loved her in. No, she would stay with the memories of him if that was all that God had wanted to leave for her.

The stranger, Moalafi, arrived in early January. He kept to himself, even refusing to sleep in the workers' houses. Instead, when the work day was through, he'd walk away down the dirt road leading from the farm, where to, he never said, but every morning he'd be in the fields working before anyone else.

'I don't like him,' Bossboy said. MmaKenny took his opinion into consideration, he'd been on this farm before she'd arrived as the wife of the tall white man they'd nicknamed RraMoleele. Bossboy was in his seventies, like her, and they had spent many a lonely night together sitting on the wide veranda wondering how they'd ever go on without RraMoleele. But they'd managed. 'He's not right somehow,' Bossboy added after a long silence.

'He's a hard worker, though.'

Bossboy sat back on the worn wicker chair and looked out over the field at the dusty red sunset in the distance. 'Hard worker or not, something's not right.'

The workers had shifted to the field planted with butternuts, now ripening on the vines sprawled along the ground. She drove out to the edge of the field, then parked and walked towards them. She spotted Moalafi working alone at the far end of the row. He had his shirt off, tied around his thin waist. She walked towards him. 'How is everything going?'

'Fine,' he said without looking up.

She shaded her eyes to look out over the field. They'd only started butternuts in that field two years before – it had been maize before that – but they were doing just fine. As she looked out, assessing the crop, she didn't hear Moalafi coming up next to her.

'He died here, didn't he?'

She jumped back a step. At first she didn't know what he meant, then she said, 'Yes, over there.' She pointed some metres away.

'He didn't suffer. It was like sleep, and before he went he pictured you in the green cotton dress at the river.'

MmaKenny looked at Moalafi, tears filling her eyes. 'Why did you say that?' she said.

'I thought you'd want to know.' He walked away, the earthy smell of his sweat lingered next to her. She stumbled quickly towards the car.

Bossboy hurried to her. 'Are you okay? You look sick.'

She fumbled with the car door, only wanting to be away from them, from him. 'I'm fine, I … I think I left the stove on.' Driving, her hands shook on the steering wheel.

How could he have known about the day at the river after they first met? About the dress?

MmaKenny waited until the end of the day when Moalafi had finished work and would be making his way down the long dirt road to who knew where. She got in the bakkie, telling Bossboy she was visiting a neighbour. As she neared Moalafi she rolled down the window. 'You need a lift?'

'No.' He kept walking.

'How did you know that, what you said about RraMoleele?' she asked. Moalafi stopped and MmaKenny got out of the bakkie. 'What do you know about my husband?'

He looked at her with eyes still and deep as history. 'He is doing well where he is. He told me that he misses you and is waiting.'

The tired, loose skin on her face sagged. 'You're lying! Why are you doing this to me?'

'They speak to me.' He stopped as if listening to the silence around them. 'He says to tell you he often thinks about the picnic on the roadside, with the broken watermelon.'

She caught a gasp in her throat. He was still here with her just as she'd always known he was. She took Moalafi's hand. It was cool to her touch. She brought it to her face and for a moment she could feel the wide, work-worn palm she had held for more than fifty years. 'Thank you,' she said, and turned and headed home.

Bossboy was waiting to help her out of the car. 'What are you so happy about?'

'It's RraMoleele, he's here with us again. Moalafi speaks with him. He is here with us, Bossboy!'

Bossboy kept quiet and looked at MmaKenny with disapproving eyes. He'd never liked that boy, and now he was putting wild thoughts in an old woman's head.

MmaKenny woke early the next day. She'd hardly slept at all in her excitement at having her husband back. She dressed and then drove out to the fields. She searched for Moalafi among the bent backs of the workers. 'Bossboy, where's Moalafi?'

Bossboy took her hand and walked her back towards the bakkie. 'I chased him off.'

'Why? Why would you do that now that we know?' she asked.

She got in the baakie and rushed towards the dirt road. She drove all the way to the end, but he was nowhere. She stopped the car. She looked down the long straight road lined with dusty trees and realised that for the first time in ten years she felt happy. The cumbersome wait of loss and uncertainty was gone. Then she remembered how Moalafi had said he would stay as long as she needed him and she realised that he had kept his promise.

The Colours of Love

HE ARRIVED with the spicy purple of the sunset, at the end of a long, hot, dusty day. They sat on the cool veranda and watched him walk up the side of the road into town.

'Where's he from?' asked Mma Boago, the owner of Mable's Takeaway, a takeaway that had never known a woman by the name of Mable.

'Don't know. What's that he's carrying?' Johnny-Boy, Mma Boago's perpetual customer and occasional bed-mate, asked, squinting his eyes to get a better look.

'Looks like a guitar. Dirty long dreadlocks and a guitar. He's not bringing anything we need around here, that's for damn sure.' Mma Boago turned and went back inside; she had magwinya in the deep fryer and couldn't waste time keeping track of unwanted strangers.

Warona was dragging her daughter, Kelapile, to the clinic when she spotted him. She wasn't one to believe in love at first sight and fairytales with happy endings, having witnessed Kelapile's father's profession of undying love just before he slipped into bed with the neighbour. It was more than being heartsore, Warona's heart had been pulled out, knocked around for twelve rounds, then placed back into her chest to perform only the bare minimum required to keep her moving. Some days she wished it would give up on that, too.

'Hurry! They'll fire me if I'm not back in an hour.' Kelapile's legs could only go so fast, decided by their three-year-old length. In frustration, Warona bent down and pulled the child up onto her back. When she looked up again, there he was.

'Do you know where I can find the guest house?'

Practical Warona didn't mention to anyone the way that her eyes went a bit funny the first time she saw him. She didn't mention the golden light that surrounded this odd stranger. It made her feel warm, and a barely-held memory flooded over her, a remembered feeling, one that she had flung away deep into the folds and creases of the grey matter of her brain to be forgotten forever. It was joy; she felt a warm, orange joy.

'Are you okay?' he asked. His full lips and kind dark eyes twisted with concern.

'I'm fine, thanks. The guest house? Come with me, I'll show you. It's near the clinic where I'm going.'

As Kelapile fell asleep on her back, Warona, with each step, fell in love with this stranger. It was reckless and without sense, but irresistible. It was a curious, spooky magic but she welcomed it.

'I'm Silas,' he said.

She smiled and said, 'I'm Warona.'

That was the beginning. The village looked on with jealous eyes as the pair flew high up to the clouds floating lazily in the silky blue sky, while the villagers stayed stuck to earth with their leaded minds and chained hearts. Resentment built against the couple and leaked out in words whispered in hidden corners and small actions made in public.

'Nothing good can come of that,' Mma Boago cautioned.

Johnny-Boy nodded in agreement. They knew only that love defined by the limits of a stingy life. Status-gaining love. Money-grubbing love. Security-seeking love. It had been so long since pure love had moved among them that all they could see was an outsider, an enemy.

Days passed. Silas played music while Warona hung bits of forest-green glass in the sunny window to create emerald patches of light that flicked around the one-roomed house. Kelapile danced. It was like that every day as they tried to circumnavigate the tricky path they'd set out on.

Silas was happy where they were, but he spoke of other places where he'd travelled, of the world out there where every step brought a new surprise and a new way to think about things. Aquamarine seas with white whipped cream waves. Brown and gold beaches. Magenta mountains. Warona would lie in his arms and listen about those magical places and Silas would rub her head, opening her mind to make space for all of the pictures he created.

But it wasn't all smooth sailing. The hovering gossip filtered through their shell of private dreams and Warona was affected. She wondered if the rumours were true. When she slipped into the villagers' way of thinking, she fought against Silas. 'Stop it!' she'd shout. 'What do you want from me? Go back where you came from, you know you will one day!' Tears flowed and she tried hard to make her heart a block of cold white ice.

Silas was not troubled by this. He knew words backed down when you faced up to them and told it like it was. He would slowly reel Warona back in, pour warm love over her ice heart, and set her back on the course they were travelling.

Then one grey day, they disappeared. All three of them. Mma Boago was cutting off chicken heads when Johnny-Boy came rushing in. He ran this way and that, his eyes wild with excitement. 'I saw it myself.'

'Saw what?' Mma Boago said as the cleaver came down with a thud, separating surprised body from instantly dead head.

'They're gone.'

'Who's gone?'

'Warona, the baby, and that stranger. They walked down the road, back into the sun from where he came. Walked and then just … they were suddenly gone.'

'Better. People were getting ideas. We don't need that kind of thing around here.' Mma Boago raised the cleaver and slammed it down hard into the wood of the chopping block.

Johnny-Boy pulled out a beer from the under-counter fridge, took a big gulp and nodded his head. Like always, he thought, Mma Boago was right.

Moving Forward

I LIE in bed and listen. I think Dad's gone — his shift starts at six and Ma's not yet awake. I get up quickly and put on my school uniform, grab my backpack and slip out into the cool morning. Today I don't feel like seeing them.

It's still early, just past six, so I wander around, killing time. I find myself heading towards Phenyo's house. I woke up thinking about her. I have an urge to see her today. While I'm walking, I think about when we were kids. We used to like to play down by the Lotsane River. There's a special place we had where a group of four flat boulders lined up in a row, hidden under a canopy of morula trees. When we were small we used to pretend it was a train. We'd take turns driving the boulders away, away to places that made us happy.

Phenyo always chose the jungle or the Arctic Circle or China. Faraway, exotic places. 'Drive me to Saturn, Boni!' she'd say, and while I was driving she'd point out landmarks. The purple oceans, the flying teddy bears, the trees made of ice cream. Her world was always big. Too big for Palapye, for Botswana. I used to be afraid it was too big for me.

Mine was always small, simple and familiar. 'Take me to Gaborone. Drive me to Joburg.' I didn't have any ice-cream trees. No teddy bears would be found when we arrived. I was just happy to be on the way with her. She'd always say: 'One day, Boni, I'll get us out of this place. You wait and see. We're going to go somewhere, you and me.'

I stand in front of her mother's two and a half. It's early but I can hear the baby crying. I wait for a moment and wonder if today might be the right day to knock on her door. Her mother doesn't like me. Last time I was there she shouted I was coming round hoping to get Phenyo pregnant again. I felt bad about that most because I saw Phenyo's face. Those words hurt her. Her mother's such a bitch, always has been, worse since the baby and all. I didn't trouble to sort her out, let her know I wasn't like that. MmagoPhenyo's not big on listening. I decide to give it a miss and head for the bus rank.

'Whatzup Littleman?' BraT says, when I come up to where he's set out his table.

'*Ga ke bue*, BraT.'

'So it's your big day, eh? A man now, 18 years old. *Maikelelo a gago ke eng?* You need to start making plans.' I'm a bit chuffed BraT remembered my birthday.

'Maybe I'll set up shop with you, BraT?' I tease.

'Ao! Littleman, you need to set your sights higher than that. Mmoloki used to say how his little brother was gonna be something one day.'

I nod but say nothing. I wonder about that, about the something Mmoloki thought I might be. BraT reaches in his bag and pulls out a small, black box. He pushes the box into my hand and looks away as if he's embarrassed. 'Here.'

'What's this?' I ask, looking down at the box.

'It's your birthday isn't it? Open it.'

I look at him but don't know what to say. BraT's been like that. It's like he thinks he needs to fill Mmoloki's shoes somehow. He's good that way and I want him to know that but can't find a way to say it without making us both feel stupid.

He looks at his watch and then up and down the bus rank. 'Wonder where Zero is,' he mutters, mostly to himself.

Nowadays, BraT and Zero work the bus rank with Find the Lady. BraT lays out three cards on an overturned cardboard box. One is the queen of hearts, the lady. The one the mark's meant to find. He flips the cards around back and forth and if the mark finds the lady then they double their money, which only happens until it doesn't. Zero acts as the back-up man just in case the mark is slow to put his money down. People are always hopeful they can get something from nothing so it's an easy way to take their money. They're just idiot fools, everyone knows the world isn't like that.

'You gonna open it or not?' BraT asks. 'I know you're gonna like it. It's something Mmoloki would have liked too.'

I like the way he speaks about my brother. I open the box and inside is an iPod, a new one. I'm touched that he thought to give me a birthday present at all, but even more touched that it was bought, not stolen. I turn it around in my hands.

'Thanks BraT. This is cool.'

'I already loaded a few songs.'

I look at him and he nods. Nothing else to say. I know what songs he's loaded for me, it's the CD BraT and Zero made with Mmoloki. They had a band: Zero on drums, BraT on keyboard, and Mmoloki on lead guitar and vocals. They played Afrojazz and pop, lots of original songs that either Mmoloki or BraT wrote. They were just starting out, but that's when everything changed.

Mmoloki knew it was coming. 'That old man's a fool if he thinks I'm going underground,' he'd told me more than once. 'This is my life. Only my life. I'm not wasting it down there.'

We were all sitting around the table that evening when Dad said, 'You start on Monday.'

We all watched him; Mmoloki, Ma and Me, letting our plates of palache and stew cool in front of us. I held my breath. It'd been building for months. Ever since Mmoloki failed his form five, Dad had been talking about getting him a job down at Morupule Coal Mine where he worked. Mmoloki hadn't said much, you didn't with our father. No one did, not even our mother. He spoke and we all listened. We pleaded our cases with Ma. She sometimes found a way to get around him, but mostly not. Mostly we just did what he told us to do to make things easier.

'I already have a job,' Mmoloki said, his hands hanging at his side. 'I made P500 last week in Gabs. I'm earning money.' Mmoloki spoke in a soft voice but I could hear the rage simmering underneath.

Dad pushed his plate away. 'Do you know what I had to do to get you that job? Do you? And then you want to sit here and be ungrateful?'

'I'm not ungrateful. I'm just not doing it.'

I sat as still and small as I could and waited.

Like he was reaching for the salt, Dad punched Mmoloki in the face. Blood spurted from his nose. Ma went for a towel but Dad stopped her; 'Sit!'

She sat back down.

The effort set his wonky lungs off and he started coughing. He reached for the water my mother handed him, not taking his eyes off my brother. His eyes as hard as rock.

Mmoloki stood up. Blood dripped on his T-shirt, making a red spot on his chest like his heart was bleeding through. He said nothing and walked out.

He was gone for most of that week, but then on the Thursday evening, after Dad drove off to the bar, Mmoloki reappeared. He must have been watching outside, waiting for the car to leave. He said he'd come to get his stuff.

'Go to your room, Bonolo,' Ma ordered me when he walked in the door.

I sat in the doorway of the room I shared with Mmoloki and listened.

'He's sick, Mmoloki. He didn't mean any of that. He didn't mean to hurt you,' Ma said. 'It's the stress and all.'

'Is it? Then why'd he punch me in the face? Why does he hit you? Don't lie to yourself, he means to hurt you just like he meant to hurt me.'

'But the job, Mmoloki. They're expecting you to show up on Monday.'

'They can expect me until hell fucking freezes because I won't be pitching up down at that mine any time soon.'

'But what about us? What about me and Bonolo?' Ma said.

'What do you mean? This has nothing to do with you.'

'It does. They're going to fire your father if he doesn't get better. How will we live? What will we do?'

I tried to hear the rest of the conversation, but they lowered their voices. I only heard Ma crying and then the door closing. At 18, Mmoloki became a coal miner just like his father. The exact thing he swore he'd never do.

I put the earphones in and press play and there's Mmoloki, singing like I could reach out and touch him, his voice so strong and clear. I close my eyes and listen and think about how much I love him. How much I miss him. I decide not to close my heart off today and I let the good memories flow over me.

Even though I left early, I'm already late for school so I decide it's better to give it a miss. The teachers give me a lot of leeway nowadays. What was school anyway, just a way to pass the time. I was certain I wasn't passing my form 5, so what's the point? I'm never going to go off to UB like the successful kids, so it doesn't matter if I'm there or not.

I head for the patch of trees behind the mall. It's the way Phenyo passes most days. I sit down on a broken brick and wait. It's been months since I've spoken to her. I miss her and I'm tired of the silence. Today I want to see her, I want her to see me.

We'd always been best friends, but then she met Tops who drove a combi and gave her money every day. For a while she didn't want anything to do with me. She only spent time with Tops. Once I tried to tell her he was no good for her, but she wouldn't listen. I knew he treated a lot of girls like that. He didn't care about her really, just like he didn't care about the other girls. I told her that, about the other girls, and she told me none of that mattered, that she knew what she was doing. Then she got pregnant and Tops disappeared. When she called him, he wouldn't pick up. Later, after the baby was born, he'd drop money at her house, money he skimmed off what he gave to the combi owner, but he didn't want anything to do with Phenyo. After that she stopped talking to me completely.

That was three months ago. Since then there's been this gap in my life, joining up with all of the other gaps. I'd see her around but she'd pretend she didn't see me. I'd pass by her house and try to get the courage to knock on the door and stop the quietness between us, but in the end I never did. Today, though, I want to see her. I want to talk to her.

I think about what BraT said too. Eighteen ought to be a special day, a changing day. Ma should have made a fuss over me. Dad should have given me a talk about being a man now. But nothing. Since Mmoloki died they're like ghosts.

I look out over the mall where people set up tables to sell tomatoes and onions. The phone ladies open their yellow umbrellas and shopkeepers unlock burglar bars. The beginning of a new day.

Before, when Mmoloki was there, everything was different. He had something, a light or a kind of magnetic pull. You felt it. Everyone loved him, you just wanted to be around him. He had enough light for the both of us. I wasn't in the dark, it was easy to see things. But then it went out. And it's been like that ever since. Like living in a murky darkness. Ma and Dad and me, just feeling around, trying to stay in the corners and away from the edges, trying to keep from knocking into feelings too big to touch. And we've just been there, not moving, for so long. I was a kid, so I waited to follow, waited for someone to lead, but no one ever did. Well, I'm not a kid any more.

I look across and see Phenyo coming. I take the earphones off. She's in her school uniform, but late like usual. I stand up and walk to her.

'Hey, Phenyo,' I say, scared, not certain if she'll see me today, hoping so badly she will.

She looks up and for a moment I think she'll walk past me but then she doesn't.

'Where'd you get that?' she asks pointing to the iPod.

'BraT gave me.'

'Stolen?'

'Nope. It's new. Look.' I hand her the iPod.

'Why'd he do that?'

I look down at the ground. 'It's my birthday,' I mumble to a passing plastic bag.

'Oh… right.' Then I can hear her remembering about Mmoloki. 'Oh… yeah.'

'Phenyo,' I start, 'I'm sorry about…' And then I'm not sure what to say since I'm not sure what I did to make her stop talking to me.

'No, no, Boni, it's me. I'm the one. I got all mixed up with everything. I let you down. I promised we'd go places, you and me, and instead I let Tops mess me around and now there's the baby and… well, I'm sorry,' she says. 'I was a fool to ever think I could do something else, be something I'm not.'

Then she's quiet for a while and I'm quiet too. I don't like that she thinks that way. It's not true. 'You can do anything, P, anything you want.'

She looks up at me, her face soft. 'That's my Boni.'

We're quiet for a while, trying to work our way back to normal. A combi passes and for a moment I think it's Tops, but it's not.

Phenyo ignores the passing combi and says, excited now, 'Hey man! You're 18! Legal and everything. We need to celebrate! Let's go and get some chicken, I'm starving. Tops gave me P100 last night to buy the baby formula. I say we make a party for the birthday boy.'

She smiles at me, that big crooked smile she gets when she's really happy, and holds out her hand. I take it and we walk up toward the junction. She's still beautiful. People at school like to say she's damaged goods because of the baby and all, but I don't think so. I think Phenyo's as beautiful now as she was the first time I saw her in standard one. I act like I don't want her to make a fuss about my birthday, but I actually do. I like that she's going to use Tops' money on me. I like it a lot.

We walk a bit and she asks: 'So how you feeling about this whole birthday thing then, Boni? Is it okay now?' She asks because she knows everything. I could always talk to Phenyo, I could tell her anything. It helped during that time.

Mmoloki had been at the mine for two months. Despite what he'd promised BraT, he never had time for the band. Any time off he spent getting drunk or stoned or sleeping. He never wanted to sing. Songs came from a place he couldn't find any more.

I was at school that day, my cake and presents waiting for me at home afterwards. It was my 16th birthday. Back then, school was good, I didn't need leeway. I was passing and teachers spoke about 'my bright future'. Mr Dithebe came into the Setswana lesson and Mma Rannoba looked at me and I knew.

I went out of the classroom and saw my Dad standing there in his work clothes, still covered in coal dust, and I knew it straight away. I knew Mmoloki was dead. I didn't need anything else. I didn't need to know that the wall of coal collapsed on him. I didn't need to know he screamed until he couldn't any more. That they weren't fast enough, that they didn't have the machine they needed, and that by the time they did it was too late. Suffocated by the coal, after two months of it choking the life out of him.

On the day Mmoloki died my father lost his air too. Like a balloon, he just deflated. Nothing was left in him. Even now. He barely talks. Where before he liked to control everyone, now he doesn't control anything.

Phenyo buys us both two pieces and chips. She's nice like that, generous and all. She smiles at me as we eat. I smile back. I used to dream about us getting married one day. I'd get a job and take care of her. We'd build a little house, maybe have kids. Where Phenyo wanted to travel the world, pulling me by the hand behind her, I wanted to stay still and quiet with her by my side.

'I wanted today to be my birthday, nothing more,' I say, when we're finished eating and just sitting. 'I'm tired of it being some sick celebration. That's all. I want to stop thinking about Mmoloki like that. He's dead. People die. People have to fucking get over it.'

I hear my voice rising and I can see alarm on Phenyo's face. 'No… sorry. It's just I've felt so heavy, so heavy I feel like I can't walk sometimes. The day comes and I feel like it's going to crush me. Do you get that, P? I think you get that, don't you?'

I need her to get it. I need someone to get it. Her, especially.

'Listen, Boni, you have the right to some happiness. Believe me, I so get it.'

She collects our rubbish and buys me an ice-cream cone for dessert. She takes a lick before handing it to me. 'For luck,' she says.

We head down to the river, to our boulder train. Seems the right place to be today. We climb up onto the large flat one at the front where the driver used to sit. It's cool from the shade of the trees. We lie back, quiet, sucking morulas and spitting out the pits, looking at the sky.

'You remember the boulder train, Boni?' she asks.

'Sure.'

She's quiet for a time. 'It was nice then. Like everything was possible.' I don't say anything but I know just what she means.

'So who's watching the baby?' I ask Phenyo after a while. I'm watching the cotton clouds drift, thinking about my happy full stomach. Thinking about how much just being there with Phenyo is making me feel better.

'My ma. She told me I'm a fool and I might as well leave the baby for her to take care of. I don't mind. The whole thing is so boring anyway.'

I can feel Phenyo's leg leaning against mine. I like it. I want to touch her thigh, but I think she might get angry. I watch the clouds and think about the fact that today is my birthday and Phenyo is next to me and how that's a very nice thing. When I woke up, I thought it would be a terrible day like always, but it's not. It's a good day.

I take the iPod out and I put one earphone in my ear and one in Phenyo's. I pick my favourite track. It's a song BraT wrote called 'Tsala ya Me'. Mmoloki's singing in his clear, pitch-perfect voice. He's singing about doing what's needed for your friend. The song is just right for that moment. We lie on the warm boulder looking up at the ocean blue sky with its sailboat clouds and I see Phenyo is crying silently.

I look at her and wonder what her tears are about. Is she crying because Tops doesn't care for her any more? Or for the baby she didn't want, or because her mother took the baby away and called her a fool? Was she crying about Mmoloki still singing in my iPod even though he's cold and dead in the ground? Or is she crying because the boulder train doesn't let her see ice-cream trees any more?

The song finishes and Phenyo closes her eyes. Her neck is wet from tears and I reach forward and wipe them away. Then she crawls into my arms and I hold her. And it feels nice, the first thing to feel nice for a very long time. I hold her and try not to think about what it all means. I hold her and think about my birthday and Mmoloki and what I'm going to do now that I'm 18. I hold her and wonder when the answers will come. And then I think that maybe they won't and I just need to keep moving forward. I hold Phenyo and wonder if moving forward feels something like this and I decide that I think maybe it does.

Acknowledgments

Some of the stories in this collection have been published previously or have been shortlisted for or won prizes.

'Eddie Fisher Won't Be Coming in Today' was originally published in the literary magazine *African Writing*.

'Pulane's Eyes' was shortlisted for the PEN/Studzinski Literary Award, judged by Nobel Prize winner JM Coetzee, in 2009 and was published in the book containing that year's finalists.

'The Lies We Can't Hide' was originally titled 'The Christmas Wedding' and won the 2007 BTA/Anglo Platinum Short Story Competition as well as being chosen for a special judges' prize, the Platinum Prize for Creativity.

'Jacob's New Bike' was first published in *Drum Magazine*.

'In the Spirit of McPhineas Lata' was included in the anthology *The Bed Book of Short Stories* (Modjaji Books) and was shortlisted for the 2011 Caine Prize for African Writing.

'The Rich People's School' was first published in *Mslexia* and has since been included in the anthology *One World* (New Internationalist).

'At times chilling, often funny and always engaging, the stories in this collection, though not strictly connected, are linked by their shared landscape – rural Botswana – and the rich characters who brilliantly portray this country's small-town life, from the old man who leaves his money to his dog when he dies to McPhineas Lata, who, from the grave, sparks a sexual revolution among the married men and women of Nokanyana village.

'In many of these stories, there is as sense that things are not as they seem: a woman's husband-to-be has a questionable past and a voluptuous stranger's beauty belies her malevolence. Characters are shaped by the particular challenges of their context – a young pregnant Mosarwa girl is forced to make a terrible decision and the barren wife of a wealthy Gaborone man is made to see an old woman with supposed powers of fertility.

'Atmospheric and evocative, these stories will entertain and transport you to the hot, dusty heart of Botswana.'

– **Bronwyn McLennan,** South African writer and editor

Other titles by Hands-On Books

A Lioness At My Heels
by Robin Winckel-Mellish

Difficult to Explain
edited by Finuala Dowling

Lava Lamp Poems
by Colleen Higgs

Looking for Trouble
by Colleen Higgs

Absent Tongues
by Kelwyn Sole